The Spirit of

The Spirit of Ecstasy

by Tony Spencer

published by

around
Yateley
publications

First published 2019

Contents

Introduction

"The Spirit of Ecstasy" is the name of the flying lady emblem affixed to the bonnet of almost every Rolls-Royce motor car made since 1911. The sculptor was Charles Sykes and he was commissioned by John Douglas-Scott-Montagu, later 2nd Baron Montagu of Beaulieu, for his own 1909 model Rolls-Royce Silver Ghost. The actress/artists' model used to pose for the sculpture, and the predecessor known as "The Whisperer", was Nelly Thornton, who worked under the stage name Eleanor Velasco Thornton. Nicknamed "Thorn", Nelly was Montagu's secretary on his publication *"The Car Illustrated"* from 1902 until her death in 1915 and was Montagu's mistress almost from the start. His first wife was well aware of the relationship and apparently got on well with "Thorn" and even corresponded with her when she accompanied Montagu abroad on their last fateful journey.

Chapter 1
Monday 15 September 1975,
12 noon

I, HARRY CRABTREE had been a travelling salesman for Small Widget Engineering & Company Limited in Birmingham ever since I completed my National Service, getting on for fifty years ago. My patch covered most of the south central and south west of England. Another salesman covered the south east, including all the Home Counties except for the plum area in the immediate vicinity of Greater London, it was the son of the principle owner of the company, a long-established family firm, that worked that rich seam of sales commissions, and would do until eventually he took over the top job from his old man.

At the time I was thinking back to, September 1975, the country was covered in tiny industrial estates on the edges of even the smallest town, with small and medium-sized independent manufacturing or assembly companies on every corner of these estates, employing mostly local workers. No matter what final product they produced or assembled, they needed self-tapping screws, nuts, bolts and washers, even the odd wood screw, to hold everything together, be they Whitworth, AF, BSF (British Standard Fine) or the new Metric sizes they were having to tool up for at the time. And Birmingham was then the centre of the world as far as manufacturing such small metal fittings goes.

Of course, the firm I worked for, Small Widget Engineering & Company Limited, was one of the best and produced a wide range of other fixings in the form of chains and latches, and could cast, press, drill or lathe almost anything in metal that a customer wanted. However, their bread and butter, as was mine, were nuts, bolts and washers, and I had to sell millions of them each year to meet my monthly quotas and targets. The bonuses I earned on new sales formed the larger part of my income, my base salary plus percentages of follow up supplies and allowances for fuel, board and food for entertaining customers was as low as they could be.

"Hello, Sir, can I help you?"

My thoughts were interrupted by the young lady with the bright red-lipped smile behind the counter in the Reception of King & Son's, a small manufacturing company of white goods on the edge of a small Cotswold town. I looked up and down the top half of the sitting girl, estimating her to be a busty single woman in her early twenties, her make-up too heavily applied for my taste, especially the mascara matted on her eyelashes which draw my attention away from her eyes. Otherwise, cleaned up, I concluded, she'd probably be quite pretty.

"Good morning, Miss, I'm Mr Harry Crabtree from Small Widget Engineering & Company Limited," I replied, with relaxed shoulders and putting on my very best smile, placing my already removed trilby hat on the counter, exuding as much calm confidence in my voice and movements as I felt necessary. "I wondered if I could speak with your Purchasing Manager this morning?"

"Do you have an appointment, Sir?"

"No, Miss, I don't," I replied, as I opened what looked like a silver cigarette case, extracted a calling card from within and handed it over to the young lady, "I noticed that your company was adverting for assembly line staff in the local newspaper that I was perusing this morning, and thought I would drop in and let your Purchasing Manager know about the best deal he could possibly find in small metal fixings."

The girl frowned, her eyes narrowed, her voice became frosty. "Our Managers don't normally see cold callers, Sir."

"Oh, really? I'm surprised," I said in a

cheerful upbeat voice, my face as wide open as a pulpit bible on Sundays, "in these competitive times, with so many small local companies like this going to the wall, you'd think all would welcome with open arms the opportunity to be in on one of the best supply deals in metal fixings going."

"Well, with respect, Mr Crabtree, that's what everyone says," the bright young girl retorted haughtily, "and our, er, Purchasing Manager won't see anyone without a prior appointment."

"No problem, then. Could I therefore arrange an appointment with your Purchasing Manager for later today or even tomorrow morning? I expect to be in this general area all this week."

"I'm afraid not, Sir."

"Ahh, doesn't he see new potential suppliers, even by prior arranged appointment, my dear?"

"No, never. We actually have supplies of small metal fixings coming out of our ears."

"Mmm. He doesn't even see anyone when it's this close to lunchtime and I've got the Roller outside ready to transport your Purchasing Manager to the best local restaurant around, you know, the smartly refurbished pub just out on the By-pass?"

"Roller?" she enquired, her pencil-thin eyebrows raised.

"Yes, my Rolls-Royce Silver Shadow V8

4-door saloon. I temporarily parked it in the empty Managing Director's slot just opposite your front entrance. You can actually see it from here. The silver and blue paintwork gleams in this Autumn sunshine, don't you think? Quite honestly, it was the only vacant space out front that was big enough to park this wonderful machine. Mind you, I can shift it in a jiffy should your MD return in the next few minutes. However, I do have a table booked for my own lunch, naturally, but it would be a very small thing to change my reservation to a table for two if I could find pleasant company to enjoy a repast with, before discussing business that might well prove to be as much to his liking as would be the meal and the comfortable ride."

"Is that the Coach and Horses you are booked into for lunch?" she smiled at me, a definite improvement in her attitude I noted.

"Indeed it is," I smiled in return.

"I cannot promise anything, but I'll see if Mrs Tremblett is free, Sir," she said, picking up the phone.

"Mrs Tremblett?" I asked.

"Mrs Tremblett oversees all our purchasing requirements. She oversees all things at King's in fact, Sir."

"Interesting."

'Damn,' I thought to myself, 'no backing

down now but, when the head bookkeeper is the one who looks after the purchasing, she's usually a sour-faced old woman who sticks to the old, tried and trusted suppliers who she has used for year on year and who have probably hiked up their prices way above the average over the course of time without her bothering to compare with competitors. Still, "she oversees ... all things" does she? That's very interesting.'

The Receptionist pressed the button on her little switchboard, while considering the man in front of her and she couldn't help herself smiling in my company. I was old to her, I knew from her look she was thinking, perhaps forty, even fifty, I imagine she guessed, but I am tall, broad shouldered, and had a distinguished bearing that I had cultivated over the years.

I still had a full head of brown hair, with an open, reasonably handsome face, my eyes sparkling with health, humour and intelligence, with a nice smile which was reflected in the crinkled lines around my eyes. I've been often told that I have a trustworthy face, which accurately reflects what I am. I hoped that what she was thinking was, that if she ever fancied going out for a spin with an older man with a Rolls-Royce motor car, she might be tempted to accompany me to lunch rather than face the boiled egg sandwich her mother had probably packed for her at dawn this morning. No, I recognised that second, softer look that she gave me, so not 'might', more like 'would'.

Idly, she turned my business card over in her hand as she waited for the call to be answered, and I could tell from her raised eyebrows that she had already admitted to herself that it was a beautifully crafted card, and knocked spots off every other of the dozen cards she'd been presented with each day over the last few years since she started working in Reception.

I smiled back at her. I always handed the cards over so they read correctly from my perspective, so the recipient has to twist the card around in order to read it. This required more concentration and manipulating, so the handler would realise that this card was no ordinary business card, but much thicker than normal and the card's surface had a really smooth quality to the touch. Technically, the twice normal thickness card was hot plate-sunk to make it dense and smooth, and the printed lettering was produced by the intaglio process, thus pressed between male and female dies, the images engraved by hand in mild steel that had to be hardened by heat and rapid cooling in a forge by a specialist craftsman before printing from, so the crisp carbon black writing was embossed at the front and indented into the back of the card. By keeping them in a silver case designed to fit them, each card handed out to potential customers was absolutely pristine, with sharp corners and no pocket lint. A very impressive card, one you might expect to receive from a Queen's Counsellor or a Lord of the Realm, not a common travelling salesman trading in nuts and bolts.

I am a man who cultivates friendships. I knew a reliable man in the printing trade, one who worked a double day shift, 6 in the morning until 2 one week, 2 in the afternoon until 10 the next, and when the 9 to 5 office staff were out of the building, my man would run off the odd private printing job for his personal customers just for a bit of extra beer money. All right, not strictly honest, but the cards were paid for and they were absolutely top quality.

"Mrs Tremblett, I have a Mr Harry Crabtree from SWE & Co Ltd in Reception to take you to lunch in his Rolls-Royce motor car ... yes ... the Coach ..." she nodded, then looked up at me, before continuing, "nuts and bolts ... screw fittings ... yes, a gentleman ... quite ... oh yes, like a shot ... OK." She hung up the phone and looked up at me again with a much friendlier smile than before.

"She'll be down shortly, Sir," she smiled a smile that went all the way up to the eyes, a reflection of enjoying the result of tempting one of her co-workers (or was it the boss?) to do what they usually actively avoided doing.

"Thank you, my Dear," I beamed, "so," I leaned in over the counter, and dropped my voice conspiratorially low, "should I be afraid of Mrs Tremblett? Does she ... does she bite?"

"Oh, she definitely bites," the girl giggled, now acting as though she was a co-conspirator with me, "but I don't think a gentleman like you should be afraid of Mrs Tremblett. Besides, she told me she's just going into the bathroom to freshen up her make-up, and that's got to be a good sign, right?"

"Ahh, so Mrs Tremblett wears make up, does she?" whispering, I leaned over even further and almost choked on the Receptionist's less than subtle cheap perfume.

"Well, not so's you'd notice," the girl divested, equally conspiratorially, "she's old school, well, not old, er, I mean she's worn well ... she can be bossy and expects everyone to jump. But..." her face noticeably softened, "when I asked for time off when my Gran was ill ... and then shortly after, when I lost my Gran, well, Mrs Tremblett was ... she was really lovely to me and gave me all the time I needed when I had to go off and cry, even giving me a comforting cuddle once, too."

"And she's in charge here? How?" It was extremely rare for a woman to be trusted to be in charge anywhere, out in the Cotswolds sticks, even in the modern 1970s.

"She's Mr King's daughter, *the* Mr King, who is the Managing Director. He normally parks where you're parked, but he's bin workin' in the London office for the past few months."

"And Mr King's son or sons?"

"They've never worked here, Sir. The company was named after a grandfather of Mr King who only had one son, and they never changed the company name. Mrs Tremblett's brothers never come in here. They was public schoolboys, an' moved onto other activities, I hear. They're probably off spendin' Mr King's money in Biarritz or Lanzarote, I shouldn't wonder. Ahh, here she is now. You won't tell her I've been a bit indiscreet, Sir —"

"Don't give it a second thought, my Dear," I smiled my trusty smile, which the Receptionist took as good a promise as she would a blessed bishop's.

She moved her lips soundlessly, "Thank you, good luck."

By then we could both hear the click clack of high heels rat-tatting down the metal steps leading from the first floor offices, the first set of stairs down to the landing out of view. We both turned to see a neat pair of black shiny stilettos hoving into view, slim ankles, shapely calves encased in sheer black nylon, leading up to a dark blue skirt, the hem hovering around the knees. As she stepped down, she placed one foot immediately in front of the other; this had the effect of swivelling her hips, swishing the cotton skirt fabric this way, then the other, as her voluptuous hips sashayed into my appreciative eye-line. Her buttoned A-line jacket, which matched her skirt exactly, disguised quite how slim her waist was while barely contained her generous uplifted bust. She had a small handbag slung over her left shoulder, her left hand holding the strap around chest high, clearly showing a prominent and expensive wedding and engagement ring set, her right arm swinging along with the extravagant motions to match her swaying hips. When her long neck and oval face came into view, I was instantly captivated.

Her face was on the long side, but that perfectly matched her long body. I estimated she was about five-ten, possibly five-eleven, even more so in those three-inch heels, her hair long and thick dark brunette with hints of red highlights. Over a delicate chin her lips were full and glossed in a light coral pink, her nose long and thin, her eyebrows thick and unplucked but the fine brown hairs had been kept neatly cut short, leaving a soft outline. Her eyes were a deep dark brown set in blinding white scleras, her dark lashes naturally defined and fortuitously nowhere near as artificially accentuated as the Receptionist's false mascara-daubed lashes. Mrs Tremblett was an outstandingly attractive early-to middle-thirties woman, I guessed.

For a moment, I regretted not asking the Receptionist anything about Mister Tremblett. But then, when it comes to business, I really am all business, I was here to do the deed and go, the deed being selling regular supplies of my company's mild steel consumables. I would have to sell myself in the process of achieving the deal, of course, my honesty in maintaining the discounts I could offer, my promises to secure a good deal, my assurances to monitor the delivery schedules and high quality of product, to be immediately contactable and responsive to clear up any issues arising from the supply or invoicing. But that was the extent of my selling myself, I was un-bribable and completely incorruptible when it came to serving my old and new customers.

"Mr Crabtree," the newcomer opened with a welcoming, beaming smile, her voice well spoken and slightly husky, one that instantly sent tingles up and down my spine but without grating. "It's an unexpected pleasure to meet you, and a welcome opportunity to dine at my favourite local restaurant."

She held out her right hand for me to take and shake.

I took it with a smile and we exchanged a very gentle handshake. It was a small, warm, long-fingered hand, her nails well-manicured and polished either with a clear lacquer or a polish with maybe just a hint of pink. I held her hand a few seconds longer than I would normally and, for just a moment, considered raising it to my lips for a light kiss, all the while looking into her warm dark brown eyes, with the slightest of Mona Lisa smiles playing upon her mouth. In her heels she was quite as tall as I was, around 6-1, so clearly she was a tall woman at 5-10 in her stockinged feet.

"The pleasure is all mine, Ma'am," I replied, and I would appreciate your advice on what would be the most satisfactory luncheon dish on offer at the restaurant, as this will be my first visit."

"Certainly, and then we can talk about what surprises you have to offer in the area of small metal fixings."

"Of course, but no real surprises, just good honest opportunities of benefit to both sides of the arrangement, I assure you. But I would hate for business to spoil a good lunch in pleasant company."

"Of course not, lunch first, business later." She turned her head to the girl on Reception, "I'll be late back Polly, and will no doubt have some catching up to do, so no more appointments today, please."

"Certainly, Mrs Tremblett, enjoy your lunch. Goodbye, Mr Crabtree."

"Goodbye, Miss, I hope to see you again, sometime soon."

I collected my trilby hat in my left hand but did not put it on.

I was definitely old school, and I regarded myself proudly as such. Having served my engineering apprenticeship over seven years on various lathes and bench drills, in a factory full of hundreds of such machines all turning out a variety of fixing widgets, required by engineers all over the world, I found that after serving my required two years in the Army, as a Sapper in the Royal Engineers, I was obliged to return to finish the last two years of my apprenticeship, compressed into a single year.

On my return I found that the younger apprentices were no longer obliged to do their Army time, so their training wasn't interrupted like mine. As a consequence, in those early months since my return, I was rusty but they were better and quicker than I was on the job, and probably better than I felt I would ever be. Now I had experienced the freedom of being outside the all-enveloping factory floor and had wider horizons on my mind. I had my pride, too, knowing my interrupted and curtailed training would always reflect in my work, so I decided to try a move into sales.

The trouble with the sales department back then, in the 1950s, was that it was almost fully staffed with ex-military officer-type gentlemen, who had never got their hands on the machinery, never had calloused fingers, dirt under their fingernails or contaminated oil on their faces because they'd scratched their noses during work. They dressed better than I did, with their suits and Regimental ties, still sporting their military titles on their calling cards, such as 'Captain this' and 'Major that'. I had to learn how to dress to impress and suppress my natural broad Brummie accent in favour of the Queen's English, and I did so.

I knew I had one big advantage over the rest of the sales staff at that time. I had the work experience they lacked. I knew how long it took to produce a million widgets, how long it took to make new patterns, test and harden the pressing dies before going into production. I could give answers to such pertinent questions, while the officers and gentlemen had to refer back to the office, or else embarrass themselves by wildly guessing and getting it equally wildly wrong. Through hard work and dedication, I was able to establish himself in the middle ranking of salesmen, never quite achieving any dramatic sales records, but avoiding the lows where my job was ever in jeopardy.

However, it was love at first sight when introduced to my three-year-old Rolls-Royce motor car and, as soon as I bought her and used her as my business car, the magnificent vehicle did wonders for my confidence and made it easier to break and melt the ice when cold calling for new business. I found sales flooded in more easily and I soon outstripped all my competitors, and remained to the forefront as top salesman in my firm.

"Would you care to take my arm as I guide you down the steps and direct you to my car, Ma'am?" as we passed through the entrance doors to the outside.

"Thank you," she said with a smile as she placed a hand on my offered forearm, "Please call me Gina, Harry, otherwise we sound far too stiff and stuffy to be able to relax and enjoy our meal together."

"Yes, it does sound much more friendly. Is Gina short for anything?"

"Yes, Virginia," she laughed, changing her overarm grip of my arm to tuck under my arm and hold my upper arm against her breast, "my older brother was three and couldn't say the whole name when I was newly arrived from the maternity hospital, so I became 'Gina' to him and it stuck."

"It suits you, it has a more cheerful, even exotic, Continental ring to it."

"And you're a Harold?"

"No. My father's best friend was a Harry, so I'm just plain Harry. Here we are."

The car was only a short way from the entrance, a gleaming two-tone paint job, silver on navy blue, parked in the Managing Director's designated spot, as I had admitted earlier, and it looked like it truly belonged there.

"It's beautiful," she breathed in admiration.

"Yes, she is," I smiled proudly as I unlocked the passenger door and waved her inside.

"Very nice, Harry, very nice indeed. It has that freshly polished leather smell."

I closed the door on her with a soft click, before scooting around to the other side.

"I'm glad you like it. I always feel special every time I get into her and effortlessly drive anywhere."

"I know what you mean, it turns a simple journey to a restaurant into more of an occasion."

"Exactly." I beamed, "No matter where I go, the drive getting there is never a chore, always an indulgent pleasure."

"So, for you, Harry, this is mixing business with pleasure?"

"Oh, I'm all business, Gina, but I do have to eat, so why not take pleasure in the little interludes in between work?"

"So no ulterior motives, Harry?"

"None of course, Ma'am ... Gina."

Now single, I had once been married for nineteen years, to Mavis Rowbottom, once my childhood sweetheart. We were engaged shortly before I started my National Service and, after I resumed work on the factory floor, we married after a two-year engagement, which was usual in the 1950s. We had two children, Gerald, who appeared on the scene just eight months into the marriage, and Sophia Elizabeth following twenty-one months after that. Gerald had gone onto university, studying history and was now teaching mathematics in a grammar school, engaged to be married in a year or so. Daughter Sophia Elizabeth had married a stockbroker and lived in Solihull in a nice suburban house and had just announced that she was pregnant with my first grandchild. My marriage to Mavis ended seven years earlier but took a whole year to go through the divorce court.

Working hard on my sales, and travelling the road from early Monday morning, and sometimes departing Sunday night for those weeks I visited the West Country, and not getting home until very late Friday evening or sometimes Saturday lunchtime, had proved a strain on our relationship. After our two children became teenagers and more independent, Mavis felt my absences even more and so she decided to take a lover.

After a two-year affair, the existence of which I had no suspicion, Mavis felt she was more in love with her lover than she was with her husband so, under the new divorce laws which made divorces so much easier to obtain, she petitioned for a divorce.

As Mavis had never worked, I had to allow her to live in the family home while the children were still in school or further education, and pay her a monthly allowance for housekeeping and generous personal use, for two years after the divorce. I must confess that I resented the payments, especially as Mavis's boyfriend moved into my old home with her immediately and, as they never married during that time, the alimony continued until it had fully run its two-year course.

Being such a stranger to my family over the years, the price I paid for being absent for so much of the children's lives, was that they both sympathised with their mother and told me directly to my shocked face that I was the one at fault in the divorce for having a career that they believed contributed to the failure of our marriage and they wanted to share no time with me after the petition was posted.

So I immediately cut himself off from my family. I never heard again from Gerald for years, except for twice briefly.

Sophia Elizabeth still sent me occasional letters, addressed to my works office as I no longer had a fixed address that I could call "home".

Sophia Elizabeth had persuaded me to give her away at her wedding four years earlier, but seeing that Mavis was there with her boyfriend on her arm, I only walked her down the aisle and briefly attended the reception after the ceremony, even though I paid every single penny spent on it. Mavis still wasn't working a full time job, so she didn't feel she should contribute a penny towards the costs of the wedding.

I left before the wedding breakfast was served and missed the meaningless cycle of speeches which promised the couple a long and fruitful marriage.

After two years, I was able to stop paying the alimony to Mavis and insisted that the family home be sold, as both the children had moved out and lived elsewhere, so it was no longer a family home with my children.

There was resentment and tears from Mavis and tearful pleas from Sophia Elizabeth to stay the auctioneer's hammer, but to no avail.

And the only other time I had spoken with my son Gerald since his sister's wedding, was him pleading with me to not sell the house until their mother reached retirement age. I exploded his stance, I was still more than twenty years away from retirement and pointed out that I needed somewhere to live too.

Gerald retorted that as I was away from "home" five or six nights a week anyway, what was the point of having a "home" lying empty most of the time. After all, Gerald pointed out, hadn't I lived in boarding houses or hotels for the past three years since the divorce proceedings started?

I still insisted on the sale, Mavis had no right to hold onto it without children in education. But I noted what Gerald had said about not needing a home base.

As a single man I really didn't need a house that stood empty four or five nights out of seven. From the five thousand pounds I got as my share for selling the family house in a nice area of Brum, I would find it difficult to get much more than a two-bedroom flat with a small mortgage and that would be left empty most of the time. No, I had to admit that I spent more of my time on the road, so it would make good sense spending the money on a better quality and more comfortable car. If I could've got away with parking a large motor home outside my customers, I might have considered that option!

℞

"You really can only hear the clock ticking," Gina marvelled, as the car joined the ring road and motored smoothly up to 60. "I thought that was just the tongue-in-cheek advertising campaign."

"No, it is a lovely smooth ride, with a powerful six-and-three-quarter litre V8 engine, it automatically glides through the gears."

"Not economical, though, surely?"

"Twelve miles to the gallon, compared to thirty in a smaller economical car, but, hey, where's the fun in those uncomfortable thirty miles to the gallon?"

"So does your firm pay all your expenses?"

"Not really, I've negotiated a weekly average which pays my board and lodgings and contributes towards my fuel and servicing costs closer to what an underpowered and rather tinny basic Ford or Vauxhall model would cost them."

"And does that include wining and dining customers and potential customers?"

"Again, not totally, but I do have a basic allowance for that purpose which has grown more generous over the years as my sales figures have improved, thanks to the tempting influence of the Roller."

"How long have you had ... her?" she smiled and I knew she was remembering me referring to the Silver Shadow as a 'her'.

"Oh, she's definitely a 'she'. She is a perfect female, demanding in being looked after so she always looks her best, she's expensive to keep, but in return she purrs like a kitten. I've had her for four years, so she is seven years young."

"So you didn't have any qualms about taking on a ... used model?" she smiled, and I imagined if that question had mixed meanings.

"Salesmen always steer clear of that word 'used', Gina. The young daughter of a friend I once gave a lift to told me that this car had always been loved, that we love her now and she was clearly loved before I had her, so she described her as having been 'preloved'."

"'Preloved', that's sweet."

"I agree, 'used' sounds like it has been all used up, that its present status is lower than it once was. No, that will never be the case. This car was already a classic when it was new, will always be a classic and will always be cared for and loved by its passengers and drivers no matter how old she is, because she will always age gracefully. She was loved, she is loved, she will always be loved. Don't you agree?" I took a moment to glance at my passenger.

Gina smiled as she returned my sidelong glance, "Totally. Sitting here I feel like a duchess."

"I think they only serve meat and two veg at the pub restaurant, Gina, not duchesses, deeply fried or otherwise. I'm sure we will be welcomed. In fact we're here."

I checked all my mirrors and signalled a right turn, turned into and parked up in the pub car park. We were early, the normal lunch trade from the industrial estate nearby had not arrived yet, so I was able to park quite close to the entrance to the bars and restaurant.

"Wait there," I instructed, "I'll open the door for you."

I strode quickly but unhurriedly around the car on my long legs and helped her step down to the tarmac. I closed the car door with a soft click and locked it with the key, before turning to face my lunch guest with my offered arm and engaging smile. She returned my smile with a brilliant one all of her own before tucking her arm once more comfortably into the right angle of mine.

Inside the pub, which had a bar off to the right and the restaurant area to the left, I said, "Just wait here a moment, Gina, I need to speak to the waitress about upgrading my original single booking."

I could feel Gina watching me as I stooped to speak with the young waitress who was almost a foot shorter than I was. The girl made an alteration in her reservation list and confirmed the request back at me with a nod and a sweet smile. I spun on my heels and returned to Gina.

"Any problem? she asked.

"No, none at all. I was booked in as a table for one at one o'clock. I just needed to bring it forward three-quarters of an hour and turn it into a table for two. They are ready for us now, or we could have an aperitif in the bar first, if you prefer."

"I think we should go through to the restaurant. I don't want to drink too much as I will have to concentrate on doing at least some work this afternoon, so a single glass of wine with the meal will be fine."

"A refreshing change," I smiled, "compared to some other purchasing managers I know," as we walked towards the girl. "Some of my customers have to be carried from the car and need to sleep it off in their offices before going home."

The girl picked up a couple of menus and waved us through to follow her with a smile.

"This way, Mr Crabtree, Mrs Tremblett, there's a table by the window overlooking the garden. It's much quieter for conversation over here." She dropped her voice as she leaned into Gina, "we put the usual lunchtime crowd from the industrial estate in the front closer to the road noise, as they usually tend to be a little boisterous anyway. The soup today is Brown Windsor."

"Thank you, Ruthie, dear," Gina said. "How's your sister? Not had a chance to walk around the works yet today and speak to your mum or even see if she was in today."

"She was back to school in this morning, Mrs Tremblett." The girl Ruthie turned to me, "My sister Tina came up in a rash on Friday and Mum thought it was the chickenpox, but the Doc said it was only an allergy. He gave Mum a cream to put on after her bath and again in the morning before she was dressed for school."

We sat down and checked over the menu after ordering a glass of house white for Gina and half a pint of best bitter for me.

"What main meal do you recommend?" I

asked Gina after agreeing that she only wanted a light one course lunch.

"This place is famous for its pies. My father loves his meat so if you are a meat eater then the steak and kidney pie is his favourite here, with mash and peas. I am not so fond of red meat, so I will go for the breaded cod with a baked potato."

I nodded to the waitress who was hovering within earshot, "We'll go with those two choices then, thank you."

"Thank you, Sir," Ruthie replied cheerfully, gathering up the menus.

After the waitress clacked away in her heels on the polished wooden floor, Gina turned to me, "So, tell me Harry, the story behind that magnificent car. Why did you buy it to use as your main working vehicle?"

"Well, I won't tell the long story, but after my divorce and the division of assets, I had enough liquidity to buy a tiny flat for one person or buy the car; one or the other, not both. I had the opportunity to buy the car and I took it."

"A step above the average salesman's car, even though you have made yourself technically homeless?"

"Indeed, the company supplies a Ford Escort Popular two-door saloon to its basic salesmen, with a 1.1 litre manual shift engine, costing about £1300 new, with between £2 and £3 service costs every month and are expected to last for around three years of heavy mileage. It was uncomfortable, noisy and tiring after a long journey through our crowded English roads, and awfully underpowered and exhausting to drive on the new motorways."

I added, "I firstly managed to negotiate a package deal of expenses on the premise that I used my own car and this was eventually agreed. So I looked around to see what car I could get for my money, considering the outlay and running costs. After looking at dozens of cars I settled on this Rolls-Royce Silver Shadow 6.75 litre V8 in silver and midnight blue, just three years old with very low mileage. I have no idea why it was sold so soon, because she was in immaculate condition. She's a beautiful car, sublime to drive and I feel like a millionaire wherever, whenever, I reach my destination. And this car, properly serviced, will last virtually forever. When I retire, I know that I could sell this car for more than I paid for her."

"You mention 'divorce' yet you still wear your wedding ring, Harry, have you remarried in the meantime?"

"No. I have not remarried. I wear the ring to give the impression that I am still married."

"Once bitten, twice shy, can't quite get over

losing the love of your life, or some other reason?"

"No, not the first two," I shifted a little in my seat and decided honesty was always the best plan. "Look. You're a young married woman, and I might take the liberty to say an extremely attractive one, so you must get 'hit on' all the time, I believe that is modern parlance for being 'chatted up'. Your expensive engagement and wedding ring set are prominent deterrents which I'm sure keeps all bar the most determined of the wolves away. My plain wedding ring similarly helps keep all bar the most determined vixens at bay. And before you say it, it's not me that's a magnet, but definitely the car that attracts them, like moths to the flame."

"Surely, it's not just the car, Harry. You appear to be a well-dressed, handsome gentleman, you're charming and very sociable, a man who looks comfortable in any company. I assure you, if you are hit on by ladies at all, it's not just about the car."

"Well, I will admit that my distinguished looks and trusting demeanour are what gets me in the door at potential customers in the first place, but I also know the nuts and bolts' business from the ground up, and that's what actually gets me the business deal once we get down to discussing brass tacks. The car helps give clients the impression that I am a much more successful salesman than I probably am, and purchase managers are often on the look out for Christmas boxes, bonus test match tickets, and free golf games before giving you a chance to quote. Well, I don't do any of those bribes, my company won't allow it and won't do it, but I do offer unique rides in a 'Roller' and the odd lunch. I believe you are the very first young Lady I have ever taken out to lunch in her. Ninety nine percent of the time, the decision makers are men of around my own age and they are simply interested in the car. If only I had five bob for every time I've had to open the bonnet!"

"So your looks and your car are more inclined to attract middle age men, eh?" Gina suggested with a laugh in her voice and a twinkle in her eye.

"Shall we just say that the procurement managers that I meet are comfortable in my company. I'm no threat to them, or their wives. There are those clients that I've known for many years who even invite me into their homes to share a decent home-cooked meal with their families while I am on the road. I love company. I love the company of men or women. I'm particularly enjoying present company, as this luncheon date has been an unexpected pleasure, but I'm really no 'lady's man', far from it. I do many business lunches and go out socially with friends in the evening, but I've not been on a romantic date with any lady, other than my ex-wife, for well over a quarter of a century. I was very much in love with my wife and I respected her trust in my continual fidelity throughout my marriage."

"And she was the one who ended the marriage?"

"It was a shock to me when she decided to end it," I said, "and I discovered that she had conducted an affair for over two years without me having an inkling, which the children only let slip after the divorce proceedings started. I even respected her right to dump me in favour of her new boyfriend and we really only had a dispute after the court rulings had run their course and the family home quite properly had to be sold."

"Polly described you as a gentleman when she called me from Reception and, when I asked her if SHE would go out to lunch with you in your Roller, she told me 'yes, in a heartbeat', and she meant it!"

"Mmm, I really find that hard to believe." I had to say. "Still, Polly did declare to me that you were lovely, sympathetic, kind and generous. And I have to say that this is the most I have enjoyed a luncheon date with a potential client for a long time."

"Well, thank you, Harry, for inviting me to join you here. They do a lovely chicken and leek pie when leeks are in season, which is my favourite. Just a hint, Harry, next time you call on King's. And, Polly can be very friendly and sweet and I do appreciate what she said about me, I suppose she was referring to her losing her Gran?"

"Yes, she was very touched by your sympathy and understanding when she had to go through that ordeal." I admitted. "Now, please tell me about yourself."

Gina told me she was a qualified accountant and had worked for her father as assistant manager at King's since her only son Giles had started boarding at prep school when he was only 7, something Mr Tremblett had insisted on as being a family tradition for the boys in the family. Eric Tremblett was Chairman of the Tremblett Group, of which King & Son were but a small part. Giles was now 13 and due home for a week's half-term holiday in October. The Kings and Trembletts were near neighbours and old family friends and she had been courted by Eric Tremblett since she was 18, after having had a teenage crush on the handsome man for years. She married him as soon as she finished her history degree at Oxford University at Somerville College, fourteen years previously. She lived with her husband in a village about eighteen miles away, but he was in a coma following a motor accident four months earlier and she didn't want to say any more about that, as it was clearly distressing to her. For convenience she was staying with her parents who lived only ten minutes away from her work. Her father was covering for her husband by running the head office of the group of companies, based in London, and I was informed that I was invited to join them for dinner that vert evening at 7 o'clock.

I said that I needed to sort out digs for the week before joining her for dinner. I had a couple of phone numbers from the local paper to try, that I had seen in the library as soon as it opened this morning. That newspaper had led me to King's.

The boarding house I usually used when I was operating in this area of the Cotswolds was unfortunately full this week. Gina said she knew of a vacancy and got up and used the pub's phone to call them on my behalf.

After her call Gina got back to the table to confirm that I was expected at the digs she'd found at 6 o'clock sharp, so I would have time to wash up and changed ready for dinner with her family, no formal evening wear, just smart jacket and tie, by 7.

Gina smiled as she looked up. "Ahh, here's Ruthie with our food."

My steak and kidney pie was nicely done, thick brown gravy, solid chunks of meat and a crisp flaky pastry topping. Clearly home made by the pub rather than bought in and simply warmed through. It tasted as good as it looked, too.

"Mmm, this is excellent. Thank you for your recommendation," I said after my first taste. "Now eat up, enjoy your meal, and then I can give you my sales pitch during coffee."

The meal was enjoyable and we had eaten it without reference to work, asking only where we came from, what interested us and we discovered lots of little things about one another.

Gina found out that I had two grown up children, but hadn't spoken to my son more than twice in the seven years since the divorce and only corresponded with my daughter by letter. I hadn't had a fixed address since the divorce started and still stayed in hotels when I got "home" to Birmingham at the weekend. I was a lifetime supporter of Aston Villa football club and was excited that they were back in the First Division again after almost a decade in the doldrums.

After the main course, we shared a simple ice cream for dessert followed by coffee before going back to the factory. Gina said she was happy to allow me to gather information about King's annual nuts and bolts requirements for my company's products.

"If you have a storeman who keeps inventory of what materials you use, all I need is to spend this afternoon with him," I said.

"Yes, Bert Brown has been with the company forever and is apparently every bit as tight with his stores as the legendary Scrooge," Gina laughed.

"I know, I've come across a few classic storemen in my time but, strangely, so many firms have recently taken the attitude that they can save costs by laying off storemen and allow staff to just help themselves from an unmanned storeroom. In no time at all, usage and wastage is no longer recorded, stock doesn't get put away properly or items are hard to find and no-one has a handle on how much stock you have, nor anticipating when items need topping up before you run out and hold up production. A good storeman is worth far more than any savings on his wages, I find."

"You'll get on well with my father, Harry," Gina smiled, "Head Office recommended laying Bert off five years ago, but Dad resisted them. It would be interesting to see how other firms in the group manage their stocks."

"I can ask him tonight at dinner. I am interested in your group of companies, does everything go through your head office?"

"Yes, all orders, invoices, payments, wages, etc, all go through head office. That's why we don't have a purchase manager as such at this factory, all procurements go through HQ. We just tell them what we need and they do the rest."

"And they are based in London?"

"Yes. Does that make a difference?" asked Gina, noticing an odd look in my face.

"London's outside my area, so any sales will be attributed to the boss's son, he's assigned the London area. I will still look after the subsidiaries deliveries in my geographic area and check in regularly to make sure everything is all right, but the bonuses are paid on where the invoice is issued, not by deliveries."

"So you'd still be servicing our account, if King's had one with you, even though you'd be unpaid?"

"Essentially, yes, but that wouldn't affect you at all, our account with you is important to the firm so you would still get exactly the same excellent service. The London office has its financial perks, but then I would hate driving round there every day, however comfortable my car is."

"Yes, my father used to take the train when he attend monthly board meetings, and work in the quiet of a first class carriage. It is only now that he has to travel up every day, that he gets driven in by car. You could do the same if you had a chauffeur to drive you," Gina laughed.

"The thought has occurred to me before while driving and I've even calculated the costs in my head, it is the cost of digs for both of us that tips that idea into the red."

"What about an amenable woman driver, one prepared to share ... your digs, and provide creature comforts?"

"Mmm, tempting thought indeed, Gina my dear, but where would one find such an amenable treasure? A lot of women my age never even learned to drive."

"You might be lucky, Harry, or you might have to train her up yourself."

"There's a thought." The pair of us laughed at our relaxed and possibly flirty conversation that we both knew was going completely nowhere, between a confirmed bachelor and a married woman and mother, but we discovered that we were relaxed and comfortable in each other's company.

We found out quite a bit about each other at

that meal. I admitted to being 45, she indirectly let slip that she was 34, which I calculated from the age she was married, how long before the wedding her son was born and the age of her son.

I was divorced, while she was married with one child, but then she admitted in whispers that her husband Eric Tremblett, the industrialist, was suspected of being a player upon a wide number of female emotions, but was in hospital in a coma in a vegetative state following a motor accident on a sharp bend on a country road.

He appeared to have run off the road and his car rammed a tree. The passenger had been identified as some kind of girlfriend, Gina admitted with a sad and disappointed expression on her face, and that she died in the accident. It has become clear that Gina had sufficient grounds to, but couldn't divorce her husband while he was in that critical condition and unable to answer for his innocence or otherwise of his actions.

"I will, in good time, divorce him for adultery, if he recovers," she said.

In the meantime she added, and this was while we were alone as we drove back to the factory, Gina set out what she was looking for in me, in addition to my supplies of screws and bolts.

"Plain and simple, my first choice after discovering Eric's cheating, was originally to take a lover for myself, Harry," she said quite bluntly as I drove out of the pub car park onto the by-pass, "or at least someone who others would regard as being a lover, as the next best thing."

"Oh." I was gobsmacked and speechless. With me on autopilot driving back to the industrial estate, Gina continued to talk rapidly, wanting to get all her thoughts off her chest.

"All right, I have slightly exaggerated, I'm not as desperate for intimacy as I may ashamedly sound. I really want someone honourable to hold my hand, someone who I can be reasonably attracted to. Harry, I need someone straight as a die who I can trust to treat me with respect. Possibly, someone who could be a potential future partner, that would be perfect but without any guarantees of commitment on my part. At the very least, though, I need an escort to functions, a companion who I feel I can rely on for advice, protection, company and, maybe, even if it is in the long run, love." Gina took a deep breath. "I do know I have looks that attract men and, even employed within the comparative safety of the Group there are lots of sharks swimming around that think I'm vulnerable, mostly because I'm a woman trying to break into a man's world of business. Those sharks simply cannot rationalise why I would want to be in a man's world at all, unless it is to play with men, to be promiscuous. That is not me, Harry, definitely not me."

I could feel her looking at me, evaluating whether I was shocked or i terested. I tried to remai impassive, silent.

"Harry, I need an escort that keeps those sharks at bay, probably because they would regard him as my lover, a lover that they know they cannot compete with, like one who drives a Roller around as his normal everyday car. I know I have only known you for ninety minutes, Harry, but I believe you are a true gentleman and I want you to consider fulfilling the role of being my escort, not forever, of course, but for the next few months at least."

"Gina, you are a beautiful woman, a truly lovely lady," I said after swallowing, taking in her beauty and sincerity with a sidelong glance. She was looking directly at me as I tried to concentrate on the road and drive safely, while considering her offer. "I know you are angry with your husband for his disloyalty, and you must be frustrated —"

"— I'm most certainly frustrated, not just sexually, but I'm also lonely, Harry, and I'm scared about my life drifting away into middle age and not having fun, companionship and ... and, yes, I fear the prospects of still being alone and having only a lone child to spoil when I reach 40 in a few years, knowing my days with him would be numbered."

"Gina," I said softly and gently, "I'm not a player, unlike your husband appears to have been. I cannot switch on and off my emotions at will. I am still, even after seven years apart, torn between my long-held feelings for my ex-wife, and my ex-children. I was rejected, in the same way your husband's affairs appear to have rejected you. We are both hurt, I would love to salve our pain but I can't help myself, I have a heightened sense of propriety. I only ever had one girlfriend, Gina, and that single sweetheart became my wife. I loved Mavis without reservation until I discovered by her own admission when I confronted her that she had abandoned my love years before and had taken another man on to share with her all her love. If she walked back into my life today I would seriously consider forgiving her and taking her back, my heart is that empty. I would never forget her betrayal, of course, but I know that at some level I still love her."

"And that is why you are such a gentleman, Harry, and why I feel I can trust you," Gina said, "please just consider being my 'go to boyfriend with no strings attached' when I need to attend a function, or want to go to the pictures, or go out with on a picnic or a walk and talk in the park with. Do you think you could do any of that for me, please?"

What could I say? One of the most beautiful mature women I've ever met wanted to go out with me, to be seen with me and through me convince her peers that I was her intimate friend? She'd even hinted at love and sex at some future point, even though those was really the last things on my mind for consideration at this point.

It suddenly hit me that for the last few years I had lost contact with my family and I really was lonely most of the time and I had never admitted that fact to anyone before, or even myself. And this was one of my loneliest sales patches, a place where I did less business, the Thames Valley and Cotswold hills; an area too convenient to the sharks of London and not too far from Brum, but I still had to cover it at least one week every quarter throughout the year. What a place to discover someone like Gina!

"Yes, Gina, I would be happy to be your friend and escort." I confirmed and confessed. "I'm lonely too, am often at a loose end in the evenings during the week, and it would be wonderful seeing more of you, even if it was unreal, all in public and on show for effect. I have enjoyed your company, and it would certainly boost my ego no end to serve you for this time, even if I turn out to be too rough a diamond for you to extend the arrangement with."

"Being seen with me might help fend off all those vixen ladies that bother you so much," she laughed, "but I think you have more than enough polish as a diamond to pull it off and put off the more competitive men vying for my attention."

"There is the point about appearing to be spoken for, to consider, and seeing you would also be a fillip to my own empty social life." I smiled in reply. "Tell you what, Gina, I'll even come visit with you at the hospital when you next see Eric, if you think that would help you cope with seeing your comatose husband a little more often. I get the impression that visiting him on your own, knowing without any doubt now what you know about his affairs, must be an ordeal."

"It is, which is why I only visit once or at most twice a week and talk to him for a couple of hours. It is supposed to help his recovery, and I now do it out of duty, not affection. His doctor wanted me to visit every evening, but I can't face that commitment to him after what he has done to destroy what I thought was a good marriage."

"Does Eric have any other visitors?"

"He has an older half-sister, a clergyman's widow, who lives in Yorkshire and can't get down very often except by train via London, once only so far in fact, but no-one else comes calling. His countless cousins don't visit. I have taken my son once, but Giles really doesn't have any relationship with Eric, he was a terrible father, and Giles had told me that he doesn't want to go again."

"Then I'll go visit Eric with you, Gina. Perhaps we can help him get out of the coma. The sooner he's awake the sooner you can get on and live your life again."

"I would love that, Harry."

Chapter 2
Monday 15 September 1975, 12.30pm

I pulled into the MD's parking space at King's again and turned off the engine.

"Shake on it?" I said, holding out a hand to agree our deal about my escorting.

Gina took my hand, but pulled me to her, with her other hand around my neck, and she kissed me softly on the lips, a long kiss that surprised me rigid at first but, as I relaxed my lips, her tongue gently probed its way in and licked my tongue briefly before she broke off the kiss.

"Wow, that's some kiss," I told her.

"Well, I thought it was important to get that out of the way as soon as possible. I know what I said by way of a shock tactic about you being my lover, Harry, and I'm not really looking for a bed companion quite yet, but I do enjoy kissing. You're a wonderful kisser, Harry, gentle and passionate without being pushy. Very nice."

"Well, it's a relief that if you're going to jump me immediately, it's just for kisses, however scorching they are. Well, Gina I do like kissing too, and that was among the most memorable of any kisses I've enjoyed."

She giggled and kissed me again, quickly, then used her thumb to wipe off any telltale pale pink lipstick off my lips, giggling all the while. "Come on, I'll introduce you to our storeman Bert Brown, so you can make a start on preparing your quote."

Bert Brown was a short, sparely-built fellow in his late fifties and had been in sole charge of the King & Son's stores for fifteen years, he boasted. During that time he had kept ledgers of everything coming in and going out of the stores. He had ledgers in the form of exercise books going back to include his predecessors long before he even started at the firm as an apprentice.

"This is great record-keeping, Bert," I told him, his records were better than I could've expected, "I can use this info to put together a chart of recent annual usage and supply for each item over the past three years."

"Oh, I've got that already," Bert said proudly, and dug out one of a number of rolls of wallpaper from a drawer. "I didn't have no paper big enough so I used the backs of these rolls. This is this year's to date."

I unrolled it and Bert pulled four metal blocks from the same drawer and held the curly roll down at the corners. I was confronted with a chart of figures, with the months of the year running down the page and across the top pairs of columns of all the various screws, nuts, bolts, and other fixings, materials and consumables supplied to and issued by the store. For each heading there was an 'in' and 'out' column, at the foot was a total, then an adjustment and a final annual stocktake figure at the bottom.

Bert saw that my eyes had reached the bottom figures. "I do a rough stocktake every month and keep a tally that I drop into the adjustment box. I works 8 to half 4 Mondays through to Fridays, but the shop floor always has evening overtime and working Saturday morning's is normal. Then, if they is behind with orders they might even works a whole weekend. The store ain't locked up so they helps 'emselves. So therefore I do a weekly rough stock take and make an adjustment. Of course, I can't take account of what stock each assembly line is holding in their toolboxes either, but as they are not held in my stock, I have to consider them issued and used."

"I see. Can I borrow the rolls covering the last three or four years for the rest of the afternoon?"

"Help yourself, mate," cheerfully replied Bert. "You know, you're the first bloke what ever bothered to ask for these figures."

"And I appreciate that you maintain them," I replied.

I took the rolls up to Gina's office. "Anywhere with a desk I can spread out and work on some figures?"

"Yes," she smiled, tucked her arm in mine and led me into the board room right next to her office, "the auditors always work in here for several days each year."

"Oh, I don't need any more than two or three hours, Gina."

I set down the rolls as well as a case containing a mobile typewriter I had brought up from my car. Gina watched me set my typewriter up with a couple of sheets of paper and a carbon paper between the two sheets.

"We have a thermal photocopier in the secretaries' office, if you would rather make a copy."

"That's all right, the carbon copy is all I need, I do a copy for myself more by habit than anything, so I have a copy I can file away in loose-leaf folders for existing and potential customers. Those thermal photocopier pages fade quickly in daylight. Do you have a facsimile machine that I could use at the end of the afternoon? I will need to send four or five pages of figures off to my office to get a price for you, otherwise I'd have to do it at the library tomorrow." I spread out the first of the charts, from three years earlier, and held down the corners with Bert's four metal blocks.

I could imagine Gina was intrigued but she clearly didn't want to interrupt. I had demonstrated that I was clearly well organised and confident that I could come up with a more than competitive bid to supply what King & Son needed and I was sure that Gina was feeling very positive about my professional approach to the process.

"Yes, there's also a fax machine in the secretaries' office, but it's quite an old one and only sends one page at a time. It's one of those things that I've noticed needs upgrading as nowadays we find we are using fax more and more often between here and head office and also increasingly with our customers."

"That's fine, thank you. I carried one around in the boot of the car four or five years ago, but as more companies started installing them, it wasn't worth paying the maintenance contract on it."

"Just use it whenever you're ready to. I'll leave you to it then. Would you like a cup of tea?"

"Thank you, I would like that, if it's no trouble."

"One of the girls usually does a tea run about

three o'clock in the afternoon, how do you take it?"

"Strong, industrial tea, with a hint of milk and two sugars, please."

"All right, I'll make sure she knows you're in here. I'm just next door, so sing out if you need anything at all."

Gina later told me that she could hear me typing away from inside her office. She said she had felt quite comforted by my activity and found herself smiling all through her own work during the afternoon. When she was finished, about quarter to five, she decided to look in on me. I wasn't in the board room by then, although my typewriter was still there. The wallpaper rolls had also gone. She went to the secretaries' office and there I was, sending pages through to my office on their fax machine.

I looked up and smiled while I listened for the tone and answering warble on the machine before pressing the 'send' button.

"Nearly all done," I said. "Just one more sheet to go after this. I've given Bert all his paperwork back before he finished for the day, so I should be all packed up and ready to go in five minutes. Are you going to give me directions to where my new digs are?"

"Even better than that, I'll leave my car here overnight and you can give me a lift in your lovely car so I can direct you there. I'll wait while you get washed and changed and you can take me to dinner at my parents' house. We don't dress formally as I said, just smart."

"No problem. If you're leaving your car here and departing with me and I bring you in the morning, won't that start tongues wagging?"

"Oh, everywhere has some sort of rumour mill grinding away in the background, Harry, and a local family firm like King's is notorious for it."

"I don't want to make you notorious, Gina."

"You won't, but I might encourage them to talk a little," she grinned, looking around the secretaries' room. It was only then that I noticed the office had gone quiet, as the half-dozen girls suddenly resumed their earlier bustle.

"Aah, then I can collect you from your parents' house in the morning, as you like, and bring you into work. I am seeing a couple of old customers later in the morning and scheduled to do some cold calling in the afternoon, so I do like to get an early start. You should get a quotation from my company in response to this fax by close of play Wednesday afternoon, so perhaps we can get back together and discuss our proposal on Thursday afternoon after you've had a chance to consider the proposal?"

"Of course, no problem. I'll get my coat and

bag and we'll go when you're ready." Gina replied.

"That's the last sheet going through now. Just need to pack up my typewriter and I'll meet you by Reception."

℞

I drove onto the by-pass again, this time in the opposite direction to the pub where we had dined and, just a few minutes down the road, I turned off as directed down a narrow country lane, which twisted and turned before rising up a steep hill. My thoughts were along the lines that this was an oddly rural place for a travelling salesman to find cheap digs.

We turned a final leafy corner and reached a pair of opened ornate iron gates, which Gina directed me to drive through, along a tree-lined gravel avenue and into a sweeping drive in front of an old Manor House, set in acres of grassy lawns, on top of a hill with magnificent views all around.

"Wow! This is like no digs I've ever stayed in before," I remarked, thinking, 'This is more like a country hotel or, is this where she lives with her parents?'

I continued speaking, "It's a beautiful house and grounds, isn't it?"

"Yes," Gina smiled, "it's lovely here."

"Where shall I park?" I asked.

"Just to the right of the main door, Harry. Bring your bags, we can walk around the side and go through the kitchen."

I parked up and took my case and a garment bag containing two suits out of the boot, along with a slip case containing some folders. There was another suitcase and a locked metal file case as well as my typewriter left in the boot, Gina noticed.

"I'll take the garment bag for you, Harry," Gina offered. I handed it over and closed the boot.

We walked around the right side of the house, missing out what I presumed were the main entrance and reception area, Gina leading the way, until we reached the kitchen. Gina opened the door and we walked into a large hot kitchen full of busy people. Gina introduced me first to a heavily-built, ruddy-faced man in his sixties, wearing a dark lounge suit.

"This is Tom senior, the gardener, usual chauffeur, but also butler and handyman, he serves the evening meal. Everybody, this is Harry Crabtree."

"Mr Crabtree," said Tom senior with a huge

friendly smile, as he held out his large hand for me to shake.

I felt a hand that was dry and calloused, the cheerful fellow towering over me by at least three inches.

"Please call me Harry." I said, "The grounds we passed through look lovely."

The man nodded with an even broader smile.

"This fine fellow is Tom junior," continued Gina, introducing a tall, thin young man wearing glasses, "he's Tom's grandson, a student at London University, and presently driving my father back and forth to the office in the capital every day."

"Pleasure to meet you, Tom," I said, as I shook the youngster's hand, which was smaller, softer and somewhat damper than his grandfather's, "what are you reading?"

"Human Geography, it's the study of people and their communities. I'm in my second year at London," he said with pride.

"This is Linda, Tom's wife and housekeeper," Gina continued the introductions.

Linda wore glasses, was also tall, slim and elegant, her dark brunette hair streaked with grey pinned up high, wearing a smart but conservative black dress, with a thin gold chain around her neck, looking every inch the perfect partner for her husband Tom.

"Hello, Linda, I hope my short notice for accommodation wasn't too inconvenient for you?" I said as I gently shook her hand.

"No problem, we always have rooms ready and available, I had plenty of time to air your room for you and put fresh towels in your bathroom. There's a bell pull by the bed that rings down here, so do call if you need anything. Bath, hand towels and bed sheets are normally changed weekly, but if you want them changed at any other time, just leave them on the bathroom or bedroom floor and I'll sort them out in the morning."

'Mmm,' I thought as I smiled and nodded, 'bedroom with a bathroom? I am way out of my league here. I always use boarding houses with a shared bath at the end of the hall, because they are much cheaper than hotels, but this is another step up entirely. Tomorrow I think that I am going to have to find somewhere else to stay for the rest of the week.'

"And last but by no means least of course, the cook Carol, who comes in four or five afternoons a week to prepare our evening meals, and for whenever there's a large dinner party," Gina said, pointing to a short, fat, red-faced middle-aged woman wearing a grubby apron and stood at a gas cooker stirring a pot. She just waved at me with a rather harassed smile on her face, so I decided not to bother her by shaking her hand.

All her introductions completed, Gina headed towards an internal door and hooked her finger at me to urge that I follow her.

"This way Harry, I'll show you up to your room."

"It's the Gold Room, Gina," Linda called after us as I followed Gina out of the kitchen.

"Oh, good," Gina said quietly as she led me down a narrow corridor to some equally narrow steps leading up to the next floor and yet another corridor, "that's the best guest room, it has a nice bathroom, with gold taps, but it once used to be the music room and for many years housed a gold pianoforte, that's since long gone. But that's where the name of the room comes from."

The room was large, with the bedside lights already switched on welcoming us inside, very tastefully furnished, with a king sized bed covered in a gold bedspread and gold curtains drawn shut at the window.

"I kept quiet downstairs, but this is not a boarding house or country hotel at all, Gina, is it? This is your Mum and Dad's house, right?"

"Yes, my parents' home, where I grew up, and this is where I have been staying for the last few months, since Eric's accident. My house is more than a dozen miles away in another village, but it's empty at the moment and I no longer felt comfortable there on my own. Harry, you are welcomed here as my special guest."

"I really can't stay here, Gina, I'm just a salesman. All right, I am hoping that your company will be a customer from Thursday, a very good customer. And I'm confident that I can come up with a deal that will save your company money, be good for my company too and possibly get me a good bonus for that first order. And rest assured I will look after your account so we'll that you will continue to get the best service you possibly can, and will continue to keep the prices attractive enough to fend off rivals year by year. But I have calls booked in with some of my established local customers all this week as well as cold calling on at least one other company every day and probably won't have any contact with your company until you receive the quote that I arranged to go through with you on Thursday. I cannot stay here beyond the necessity of tonight, as it is too late now to find anywhere else. You can see that, surely Gina?"

"You are here as my personal guest, Harry. You're my escort, remember, we have shaken hands and even kissed lips by way of agreement on that. I have spoken to Linda, who has aired this room for you, and have fully explained your presence here to Mum and Dad. They are expecting you to stay here for as long as you like and join us daily in our evening meal. Put your case down next to your garment bag on the bed. ... There, that wasn't too hard was it?"

I did as I was told, turned and presented her with arms held out and palms upturned as if to say, 'what now?'

And Gina simply stepped into the space between my arms, wrapped her arms around my neck and open-mouth kissed me on the lips and inserted one knee between my legs and rubbed her provocative thigh firmly against my groin, while her tongue tried to worm its way past my lips into my mouth.

My jaw clamped shut so Gina's insinuating tongue couldn't get past my teeth. I put my hands on her upper arms, gripped her gently and pushed her away, breaking lip contact until she replaced the sole of her errant leg back on the carpet next to her standing leg.

"Gina!" I wailed in exasperation, "you're still a married woman!"

"And you are still a gentleman, a man of principle, Harry," Gina smiled, her head slightly tilted to one side as if she was examining me from a slightly different perspective, "I respect that enormously, but I also felt I had to test you."

"Test me?"

"You are indeed a gentleman, Harry, just as I thought you were after I tried to throw myself at you earlier in the company car park. A woman finds it hard sometimes to tell the difference between a cad and a gentleman, but after my bad experience I think I can now tell the difference."

"And what is that difference?" I asked, still holding this lovely lady at my arm's length.

"Well, when I was younger, I didn't know any better, so unfortunately I was charmed by and ended up married to a cad, an absolute cad actually, and then I had to make the best of a bad choice in husbands and am determined to avoid repeating that error. Harry, you must know that I have been 'hit on' and flirted with continuously ever since I was about 15. And I still am today, even with my expensive ring set that marks me out as a married woman. What I didn't know about cads and gentlemen back then has been more than filled in since, so I was confident that you are exactly what you seem to be and my kiss here and now in your room proves it."

"Proves what?"

"Proves that your body is naturally capable of reacting automatically to my kiss and the stimulation of my rather unsubtle knee pressed into your groin. I felt your arousal so do not deny it. We are in a private room, out of earshot of the kitchen and the living rooms, yet you resisted your natural hormones and refused to ravish an apparently willing female, because of your morality, your sensibilities. I'm certain that Eric would've had no hesitation to do what comes naturally in the same circumstances. Tell me honestly, Harry," she added softly, "after nearly twenty years of marriage and being a single man for the last six or seven years, exactly how many women have you bedded in your life?"

"One," I replied without even having to think about it, "only one ... ever. I told you before I was no player. I played for keeps and I lost."

"So you married your childhood sweetheart, Mavis, and lost your virginity to her, yes?"

"Yes. I did."

"Well, so did I. Relax, my dear Harry, I repeat my proposal for you, with a minor adjustment. It will fill your evenings and, hopefully, most weekends and provide you with a secure and above average home base."

She placed the palms of her hands on my chest and stepped close into me. I had already relaxed my grip on her arms.

"Do you want me to tell what my proposal is in more detail, Harry? And the rewards?"

"Why not?" I replied with a question.

"Why not, indeed, Harry." Her palms climbed my chest until one rested on my clavicle and her right palm cupped my jaw, her index finger gently stroking my cheek. "I have needs, Harry," she teased with a smile.

"Geeeena!"

"Just teasing, honey. I told you that my 'loving husband' is in a coma. What I didn't say is that he is unlikely to ever wake up again. They have recently fitted monitors that somehow check for brain waves or something and they're not picking up anything. He is in what they call a 'vegetive state', brain dead. He cannot move, barely responds to external stimuli and cannot breathe on his own without air being pumped in and out of his lungs. His heart is beating but the doctors say this will stop shortly after they turn off the respirators."

"I am so sorry, Gina."

"Don't be, Harry, he is the cad that I married as an innocent, and the accident that he barely survived proved it."

"Proved he was a cad?"

"Eric was not alone in his car when he wrapped it round a tree at an estimated ninety miles an hour. A young married lawyer, in her twenties and in his employment in the group legal office at head office, was dead when she was pulled from the wreckage. As well as suffering impact injuries from not wearing a seatbelt, she was suffocated to death by swallowing whole the top three inches of Eric's erect penis, which blocked the airways in her throat, while Eric was bleeding out, partly from the stub of his engorged dick that she left behind, and massive internal injuries. The prognosis is that in the throes of ecstasy, Eric must've closed his eyes and lost control of his Bentley, left the road and on impact with the tree, the poor girl, who was already in the act of swallowing his dick, she bit it off and swallowed Eric's little head and a bit more."

"Blimey!"

"Yes, it made headlines in one of the less respectable Sunday newspapers yesterday. So. In the absence of my errant husband, I have need of an escort for formal functions a couple of times a week. Someone to take me to the ballet, charity balls, dances, parties, and the like, especially in the run in to Christmas and the New Year. I'm only interviewing you for the job, Harry, you have no rivals, no competition, just yourself. There will be some fringe benefits on offer, if you want them. Are you interested in the job?"

"I don't know, Gina. What does Eric's family say?"

"Other than his half-sister who agrees with

me, the rest of his family are being a pain in the arse, Harry. This is why Eric's life support has not yet been switched off. The cousins have taken out a court procedure preventing action by the hospital for another two months and the lawyers say that could be extended through another action by a month or more before we get the say-so to turn off the life-support."

"If he's brain dead, what is the point of keeping him 'alive'?"

"Exactly, just what the doctors are saying. But, all the while Eric is technically still alive, the rest of his family can prevent the reading and actioning of his Last Will & Testament, a copy of which indicates that everything goes into a trust for Giles, which will mature when he is 28, in 13 years' time. Until then I would be appointed as a trustee to look after Giles' interests, to administer the assets, which includes half a dozen businesses. All of them are run by his relatives who are afraid for their jobs once I am able to take them over. Most of them are useless managers and only got their positions because they blackmailed Eric by their knowledge of his extra marital activities."

"And you can't take over control of the assets until after Eric dies?"

"Correct. I cannot in any case use the assets for my own benefit, as I have guarantees of income provided elsewhere in the Will, but the assets need constant attention because, in the meantime, I am sure some of these cousins are furiously lining their own nests in what little time they have left in charge. I wonder if there will be anything left over for Giles' future." Gina said. "Now, get washed up and changed, I'll come back for you in twenty minutes, unless you need help dressing...."

"Go on, off with you, you minx. Come back in twenty."

When Gina collected me twenty minutes later, I had showered in the impressive gold-tapped bathroom and changed into my smartest suit and shiny shoes. I know she said not to dress up for dinner but I assumed she meant no evening wear, just a lounge suit or jacket. And I was glad I had.

Gina was in a figure-hugging electric blue dress, sleeveless, held up by tiny straps the width of noodles, and cut off just above the knees in the modern style that perfectly showed off her curves, and shapely knees and legs above three inch heels. Her thick dark brown hair was piled up on the top of her head making her look even taller. A single string of pearls around her neck and pearl stud earrings completed the picture of elegance and beauty. She really took my breath away, leaving me with uttering a gasp at first sight before she smiled, knowing that I was more than suitably impressed, and held out a cocked arm as she half turned, offering a profile that alone that would have rendered me speechless.

I gladly took her arm and, wordlessly, she led me in the opposite direction to the way we had come down the corridor, leading to a landing and via a grand staircase down to the entrance hall.

Gina led me into a classic dining room with a long mahogany table that could easily seat sixteen, but tonight set for just four places at one end, not far from a roaring fireplace. Standing by the fireplace, warming themselves, was an older couple, probably in their sixties, I thought, who were quite elegantly dressed for dinner.

"Harry, my parents Alfred and Pamela King," introduced Gina as we approached the smiling couple. "Mum and Dad, this is the gentleman Mr Harry Crabtree from Small Widget Engineering & Company Limited that I was talking to you about earlier."

Wearing a brilliant welcoming smile, almost

a replica of her daughter's stunning smile, Mrs Pamela King stepped in front of her husband in order to greet me first, ignoring my outstretched hand to reach up to grip my shoulders rising on her tip toes and pulling me down to kiss both my cheeks. I had to stoop to her five foot five, which I estimated her height to be. Her hair was dark streaked with grey, particularly where her parting on the right side of her head was, refreshingly natural but beautifully cut and coiffured. She had also chosen pearls for her adornment, a longer necklace of three strings, and wore a more conservative black dress covering her knees, long sleeved and with a round neck covering up her upper chest.

"Lovely to meet you, Harry," she said in a soft, cultured voice, her eyes sparkling, full of intelligence and apparently genuine pleasure at meeting me, "please call me Pam. I do love the colour of that suit, so very sharp and modern."

"Thank you, Pam, it is both an honour and a privilege to be welcomed into your home."

"You are most welcome, please do make yourself at home, both in the house and in the grounds during your stay here," Pam smiled.

Then she stood to one side to allow access to their guest by her husband. He was very tall, two or three inches taller than me and much thinner. His hair was almost white and quite thin on top, I re-estimated his age to more like seventy than sixty. He was blessed with a disarming smile, lively grey eyes and a firm handshake which he executed with both bony hands, dry and warm from the fireplace.

"Pleasure to meet you son, heard lots of good things about your company and particularly the way you do business, so we are looking forward to having a long and fruitful relationship with you. Call me Fred, Harry, everyone else does."

"It is a pleasure meeting you too, sir, er Fred, I wasn't aware you even knew of my company," I replied.

Fred maintained his grip on my hand with both hands and winked at me. "Soon as I heard you were coming here tonight," he confessed, "I phoned round a few likely customers of yours and picked up more than a few glowing reports of your service. Research, my boy, is essential in any business, that and having the right contacts when you need them. Your reputation goes before you, what people say about you, and how enthusiastic are the answers given, well, they do you credit, son. Now, what's your poison to be before dinner?"

Fred waved his hand across a table which had a dozen bottles of booze, sherries, brandy, gin, dark and white rum, bourbon and whisky, including a Glenfiddich and a Laphroaig, 8 and

10 year old respectively.

"I'll have the Glenfiddich with plenty of water, please Fred," I said, "the Laphroaig is more for after dinner, I think."

"Oh we have a different table in the library for after dinner drinks. If you like highland whisky, we have a rare Blair Athol 13, which only requires a single drop of water to reveal its many rewarding talents. Something special to look forward to."

"Sounds perfect. I've enjoyed the 10 year old once before, but never come across the 13."

"You're in for a treat later then," Fred said as he poured a generous three fingers each of the Glenfiddich into a pair of cut glass tumblers and splashed in a little water, before handing one over to me, "I have a few shares in Arthur Bell's distillery which I delightedly inherited from my father, so we get offered a case of these rare treats from time to time."

Meanwhile, Pam had prepared two small gin and tonics, with ice and lemon, for herself and her daughter.

"Well, chin-chin," declared Pam and we all raised our glasses in the air and swigged what was for me a burning mouthful.

Then Pam tucked her free arm into my free arm, saying, "Let's walk around the room and have a private talk, my dear boy, while Gina and Freddie talk about today's boring everyday business in their respective offices."

"Certainly," I concurred and we set off around the room at a funereal pace, with Pam occasionally stopping for a moment here and there.

"What do you know of our Eric Tremblett, Harry?"

"That he is on life support with little hope of recovery, has only half his manhood left to boast of and, when he was er more intact in that area, he earned a reputation of waving it about a bit, and now the sharks in the shape of his cousins are circling the hospital bed."

"Ha!" she laughed, "Good boy, I had the impression you were just as sharp as your suit. Now, what do you think about my daughter Gina?"

At this point Pam stopped to look closely at me. I stooped to move my lips nearer and spoke with a whisper.

"Your daughter is ... lovely, but what she is asking for from me seems ... well, desperate, far too desperate for such a beautiful woman. Why does she need an escort, for one thing, and why me for another?"

Pam smiled and, with a little tug, set us off walking again. I resumed my upright position and simply went with the flow.

"My daughter is, as you say, lovely, not just with skin deep beauty but is a lovely person through and through. She deserves happiness, but she finds herself in an invidious position, Harry, in fact we all are. Freddie was due to retire in the next few years, leaving Gina to run King's for the next five years or so, to prove to herself and others of her managerial qualities, before stepping up to the main board and become vice-chairman of the group under her husband. Eric is quite a bit older than her and had been expected to run the Tremblett Group for another five to eight years at most before allowing Gina to chair the group until she was say, fifty to fifty-five. By then their only son Giles would be experienced enough in the workings of the Group and ready to take over the family business, so the Trembletts Group would continue running with a Tremblett at its head. It is Eric's wealth that holds the group together but it's Eric's accident that has put the kibosh on the timing of those plans."

"Is there no one else to run with the ball for a while, say the current MD of one of the group companies?"

"They're all Eric's first and second cousins, that Eric hand picked because he knew he could manipulate them. They're universally corrupt with the morals of mountain goats and almost completely useless as businessmen. They could never work together as they are too suspicious of each other. Eric was a ruthless bugger who felt he had to control everything, including allowing them each some salacious material that they thought they had on him, but knew they could only use once, but were never allowed to be in a position to maximise the effect of what they had to benefit them. Eric's control on internal politics meant the group was Eric's powerhouse and therefore was never allowed to achieve its full potential. Gina and then Giles, both being Trembletts, were going to be the saviours of the group."

I wondered why Pam was the one telling me this and not the two business people standing by the fireplace. Now we were at the other end of the room and turning so that we could now see the pair and, every time I looked up, it appeared Gina was watching us closely.

"If the Trembletts are in all the key positions, why isn't one of them doing Fred's temporary job?"

"Ah," Pam smiled, "Because none of them will allow any one of the others to take over even temporarily. Eric has individually manipulated them for so long that there is no leader and most of are so insecure at full board level that they prefer the safety of their own domains.

This was why he planned to step down in favour of Gina, while still expecting to be in the background, maintaining control through Gina until Giles was up to speed. Freddie had been Deputy Chairman of the group for many years. Gina will almost certainly be promoted to the main Tremblett Group board this week, to temporarily fill Eric's vacancy, but she will need support at work and after work. We are still at a point where very few women are successful in boardrooms, Harry, there are too few of them, so they are isolated and easy to gang up on and outvote so they often feel victimised and some actually experience becoming victims. This is where you come in."

"So, this is why they are collectively delaying switching off poor Eric's life-support, I suppose it delays the inevitable of Gina stepping up to the board and eventually becoming chair. The sharks smell blood in the water and see a chance to take Eric's place?"

Pam stopped again and pulled my arm down again to kiss me on the cheek. "I think you are sharp enough that you are going to enjoy these next few months, that is if you want to come on board."

"I already have a job," I said quietly.

"And of course you have and you must keep it and maintain your high performance in your job. This is only a temporary part-time situation, but for the right person the possibilities are tremendous. You are completely independent of King's and the Tremblett Group and known to be incorruptible. Freddie knows a lot of people, he has stepped down from being on many boards and trade association bodies in recent years, readying himself for retirement, so you will find your additional new sales adding up with very little extra effort on your part, so leaving you free so you can physically and socially support Gina as she establishes control and builds up her confidence dealing with the directors of Trembletts. Maybe, down the line when Gina and Giles are in control of the board, you may find yourself appointed to the main board at some non-executive level. You have a great opportunity for professional advancement if you prove yourself worthy, as we are certain you will."

By this time we had worked our way around near to the start, and Gina glided over to take my arm from her mother.

"My turn to walk you round," Gina laughed and we started to circulate along the same path. "I thought you looked so handsome on my Mum's arm and, when you bent down to speak in hushed tones, I couldn't help but be a little jealous of my mother."

"Gina. Any room that you are in, you need never be jealous of anyone, even your mother. In that dress, with your smouldering beauty and your present air of self confidence, you outshine us all."

"I have only really felt this confident today, Harry," her dark eyes burning into me, "because I think you could make all the difference, for a number of reasons."

"What reasons? Because I am completely out of my depth here, Gina, I'm nothing but a simple screw maker from Brum."

"No, my dear Harry, you are so much more than that. You have the common touch, people of all classes like you, trust you, and believe in the value of what you say. You are confident with being brash and you own and drive a Rolls-Royce like you deserve to, Harry. No one can knock you, because they assume you are a success by association with that lovely car. Purchasing officers are flattered that their business is important enough for your company to send their best man to see them. Then, when they meet you, they find you're honest and friendly, you don't need to do the hard sell, because you exude that confidence that you've already made it. Your customers truly believe that you are getting them the best deal ever because they know you don't need to bust a gut to achieve sales figures in order to keep your job. They understand that you are the top man and they truly believe that what you are offering them is the best they'll get anywhere."

"But they do, they really are getting the best deal, my company really have got the process absolutely right," I insisted, trying to appear hurt by her analysis.

"And you are right, your company do get it right. We do too, so we can recognise and appreciate someone else that does business the right way. Dealing with you Harry, everyone gets it without having to think about it too much. Bert thinks you get him and that you appreciate his stock control system on his rolls of wallpaper and you're the only person in 15 years that has recognised and praised his record keeping, the rest of us, we who work with him, employ him, simply took his efforts for granted. I met Bert on his way out today, timing my walk to the time clocks for the end of his shift, in order to have a quick but casual word with him; he thinks you walk on water, Harry. Two of my friends joined me in the loo at the Coach & Horses and told me they would cheerfully carry your babies full term and pass them off as their husbands' offspring and just hope the babies look like the mothers."

"Poppycock!"

"No. True. Our young waitress wanted to introduce you to her Mum and even she said she'd take you home for herself if her Mum didn't want you! Did you notice when you were in the typing pool and faxing those five long pages to your office, that no keys on their typewriters were being struck until a few moments after I walked into the room?"

"No," I confessed, "I didn't. I was concentrating hard on putting the pages in the right way up."

"And now, Harry, my dear man, walking round this room with me on your arm, you've looked at my eyes almost the whole time and not once stared down at my cleavage."

"Well," I laughed, "I saw every inch of you when you collected me from the room and I have a very good memory for what I like."

"See? Harry, you are a funny, charming man and excellent company —"

"— for an escort?" I smiled and this time I first deliberately established eye contact with Gina before focusing my complete attention on her magnificent cleavage, relaxing my jaw and letting my tongue hang out loosely.

"Harry Crabtree," Gina giggled, "If I didn't have a drink in my hand I would slap you silly!"

I looked up at her and took in both her eyes again as I moved closer. "No you wouldn't, Gina, you'd be kissing me instead."

I leaned in as I slowed down the pace of our walk and pressed my lips lightly against hers. She shivered and then returned my kiss and our tongues touched for just a moment before I broke off the kiss and smiled at her.

"I want to come on board, Gina, just tell me the what, when and where of whatever you want me to do. I'm your man, I'm your escort."

℞

The meal was hot and excellent, I thought, and efficiently served by both Tom senior and Linda. The conversation was light and relaxed between the four diners.

Gina's father Fred admitted to me that he wanted to retire soon but had no son willing to take over his stewardship of King's and certainly not that of The Trembletts Group. King's joined The Tremblett's Group in Eric's father's days and, while King & Son's could survive on its own, it would initially suffer outside the Group and might be forced to merge with a rival.

Fred explained the company had always been King & Son rather than 'Sons' because the founder, Fred's grandfather, had only one son, Fred's father, and the next two generations did nothing to change the name. Fred and Pam's eldest son was 40 and a lieutenant-colonel in the Army based in Germany, hoping to be a general by the time he was 50; while the youngest at 32 was a racing sailor based in Australia who never wanted a desk job or indeed ever wished to return to the UK to live.

So the middle child of the brood, Gina was, as a qualified chartered accountant, being groomed to take over first the company and then the group board. As her group chairman husband was now in a coma, her Dad as deputy chairman was the most experienced group board member and was standing in as temporary chairman.

The plan was to invite Gina onto the group board to fill the vacancy left by Eric's incapacity and give her two or three years to learn how all the different businesses operate before taking over the main board from her father. There will have to be a major shake up of all the company management teams to flush out the Tremblett makeweights and bring in or promote fresh talent.

Giles Tremblett was only just in his teens and, because Eric took little interest in him, he had largely been brought up by Gina and the King family and was turning out to be a bright and well-balanced young man, who would one day be expected to run The Tremblett Group.

"So, where exactly do I fit into this scheme of things?" I asked.

"Ordinarily," spoke Pam, sitting opposite me, "in the circumstances of Eric's crash, and the subsequent Coroner's verdict of 'death by misadventure' of Mrs Alice Couples, a 28-year-old legal advisor to The Tremblett Group board, and the public knowledge that, although she suffered internal injuries that might inevitably have led to her death, the actual cause of death was asphyxiation due to a substantial part of Eric Tremblett's anatomy completely blocking her airways, Gina would be quite within her rights to divorce the cad."

"Unfortunately," Fred King, sitting diagonally opposite me, continued, "her husband is still in intensive care four months after the accident. The knowledge of his infidelity only became public knowledge at the Coroner's Inquest just over a week ago. Therefore, it would be in very bad form personally and for confidence in the business to first pull the plug from the marriage with a messy petition for divorce and then, secondly, to physically pull the plug on his life support before the ink was even dry on the petition. Even if she filed now, Gina would still technically be Eric's wife when the life support was switched off, as the average length of time to obtain a degree nisi is nine or ten months."

Much of Eric's medical difficulties came about," Gina contiued, "because of the blood loss from that severed member plus a multiple fracture of a leg, which ruptured an artery, and internal bleeding. This resulted in less blood reaching the brain before the emergency services got onto the scene, to staunch the blood loss and get him onto a drip and restore blood pressure. Although there were hopes in the initial stages that he would wake up and begin to recover normally, or with perhaps some limited impairment, the latest medical opinion is that he's essentially brain dead. This leaves us with a problem. The rest of the Tremblett family need Eric alive to maintain the fine balance between the group companies, so they don't want that lifeline plug pulled or at least would like the prospect stalled for as long as possible."

"Gina has been visiting her husband once or twice a week now for the past three months or so," Pam continued, "after spending the first two weeks virtually at his side, which is two weeks longer than that cheating bastard deserved. The doctors are saying there is no hope of recovery, and been saying for over a month now that he will die as soon as the life support is turned off as there is simply no sign of brain activity. This means that, although Gina can't suddenly cohabit with a new partner, there is no reason why she can't begin to enjoy a social life again and start seeing someone reliable and respectable for dinner dates, at social functions, the theatre, go to business meetings with, etcetera, and have someone to support her at board meetings and accompany her on the factory site visits which she will need to do once she's voted onto the board." Pam beamed at me. "And this is where we hope you will come in, Harry."

"Why me?" again I asked, "I don't move at all in polite society. Basically, I'm a homeless travelling salesman, literally living out of a suitcase. While I am not averse to a little culture now and then, I don't go to the ballet, the theatre or Ascot Week, I'm a season ticket holder at Aston Villa FC for goodness sake!"

"Did you know," Fred smiled, "that The Tremblett Group has an executive box at Highbury, Harry? Has Villa played The Arsenal yet this season?"

"Yes, we beat them 2-0 at Villa Park only last Saturday. I think we're due to play down at Highbury in early January, the second weekend, the tenth I think."

"I'll sort out a couple of executive box passes for you," smiled Fred, "I might even get a couple for Pam and I, as support for you."

"The reason 'Why you' is because you are a sweet and charming man, Harry," Gina spoke up, turning in her chair and looking me directly in the eye. "And that's not just me saying it, we've done our research this afternoon and everybody you work with likes and trusts you." She started counting off on her fingers, "You're relaxed in company, you look as though you are enjoying meeting my parents here in this house, when most people would be somewhat cowered by it, but you're not. You are confident without being cocky, charming but not smarmy, amusing but inoffensive, honest and we clearly know from customers we've spoken to that you have a high integrity rating for someone in sales. I don't know why your wife Mavis gave up on you, unless she is a fool, but you are what any woman would call 'a catch'."

"I was mystified too, when she asked for a divorce. I must say it was the worst moment of my life."

"You are now single after a long marriage, but it was your wife that strayed and deserted you, not the other way around, which is far more common," Gina said. "You do not possess that obviously predatory eye that so many divorced men develop, which makes you a sweetheart in every woman's opinion. You also drive a beautiful Rolls-Royce as your everyday car, which shows impeccable good taste. So, at first glance, you would not look like you're seeing me simply as a means of getting hold of my family's money. You are not on the board of any of the group companies, or our competitive rivals, and therefore you're no threat to the Tremblett family and their allies. You may be selling yourself short here by admitting to be a simple salesman, living out of a suitcase, but we know that you have worked for a very respectable company ever since you left school, other than the two years when you proudly served your country, which makes you reliable and dependable. Honestly, Harry, you are the most perfect escort I could wish for."

"And you would not be out of pocket, Harry." Fred assured me. "You can live here freely, use this house as your base for the northern half of your territory, and King's will happily pay your boarding costs when you have to work too far away from here in Devon and Cornwall, which is the distant part of your area; we'll just set up a dummy company for you and pay your accommodation bills through our books as consultation fees. Hopefully we may only tie you up in this arrangement for between three to six months."

"And I will even gladly wave you off to Aston Villa on Saturday afternoons," Gina smiled, "so long as you're back to me in time for any parties or events we might be invited to as a platonic couple with no overt public displays of affection, at least until after poor Eric fades away."

"It does sound like you don't love your husband any more," I observed.

"Eric had been guilty of adultery throughout our marriage. I soon suspected him of it, especially as he was cold to me in recent years, but I never had any concrete proof. He was on his own a lot of the time, stayed away overnight two or three times a week, pretending that he had meetings, and we had stand-up rows about those unsubstantiated rumours which I continually heard about his reputation with mostly young vulnerable women. He would never admit to affairs and I never had any real proof. But over the years it was quite obvious that I was no longer as attractive to him as I was before we had Giles, and I in turn gradually lost my attraction to him and any respect for him evaporated away. Although we slept together in the same bed four or five times a week and Eric initiated sex some of those times, it wasn't what I would regard as lovemaking. He was the type of man who took want he wanted and resistance was futile. I didn't resist him, I just let him get off so it was over soonest. Sorry, Mum, Dad, too much information, I know, but at least he never beat me up or anything. He was just a disappointment to me and there was no love there between us any more. I wasn't free to simply up and leave him because of Giles and the power Eric had of parental access."

I noticed her eyes watering, so I placed my hand over and held her hand while at the same time passed her my napkin.

Although she had just said that there was no love between them, I was sure there must have been more than enough to bring to mind regrets about her private life. With the experience of my broken marriage I could understand what she was going through.

She glanced sideways at me while I changed the subject.

"Thank you, Fred, Pam," I said, "that was a wonderful meal, I would really like to pass on my thanks to Carol in the kitchen. Rarely have I enjoyed a meal so much."

Tom senior, who had just entered the room and was standing by the wall, coughed, "Excuse me Mr Crabtree, but Carol has already gone home to her family for the evening. She always does as soon as the last dish is served up."

"Thank you, Tom," I replied, "l hope I'll see and thank her personally tomorrow before we go off to the hospital, but if not I would be grateful if you could tell her that this is the best home-cooked meal I've enjoyed this year."

"I will, Sir, thank you," smiled the servant,

who until then had silently waited on us impassively throughout the meal.

"Carol is a wonderful cook, Harry," Pam smiled, "I have always felt that we are really quite spoiled by her."

Gina pressed her other hand on top of mine, "And that is another reason everyone likes you Harry. Our meals are always this high standard and no less even when we've hosted large parties, but hardly anyone ever acknowledges the cook and no one has ever remembered her by name, and you've only been introduced to her a couple of hours ago."

"Well," I smiled, "the artist creating such a memorable meal should be remembered."

Tom coughed and then spoke up as the conversation paused, "Coffee is now ready in the library."

"Thank you, Tom," Pam said, "Gina and I will take our cups to the evening drawing room for ten minutes, if you don't mind, gentlemen."

Both Fred and I acknowledged the instruction with nods. I immediately thought, 'This is where Fred sets out the restrictive ground rules with Gina or else sends me packing.'

I stood up as soon as Pam and then Fred rose, Gina released her hands but as soon as she was standing she tucked her left hand into my right arm and enclosed her grip with her right, pressing her soft breast into my upper arm. We edged sideways past our abandoned chairs and moved towards the door that Tom preceded us through, and were waved in front of her parents by Fred.

The substantial library was a smaller and cosier room than the dining room, again with a log fire burning in the grate, fresh logs stacked in a cast iron lion by the side. There must be an endless supply of logs to burn from the estate, I thought.

There were eight comfortable armchairs, five of them in a semi-circle around the fireplace, a central round table in the centre of the room with four hard chairs around it, and a couple of small desks each with a hard chair tucked in against the wall.

One and a half of the walls were completely covered in books, floor to ceiling. The coffee pot, cups and saucers, sugar and milk were on a silver tray on the round table. Pam prepared coffee for herself and Gina, then the younger woman seemed reluctant to leave me behind before she followed her mother through the other door.

"How do you take your coffee?" Fred asked me when we were alone.

"Black, two sugars, thanks," I replied, "So, now that we are alone, Fred, what is your take on Gina's crazy idea of having me or anyone as an escort for her?"

"Actually, this was Pam's and my idea. Look, take a seat by the fire and I will explain...."

Once we were settled he continued.

"Gina is a competent businesswoman and confident leader and she is doing great at King's, where she has stepped up and taken charge for the last four months and everyone already respects and loves her. King & Son's is still run as a family firm within a loose group of associated companies. The individual companies in the Group all hold a minimum two-and-a-half to a maximum five percent share of the holding company and the holding company owns between a fifth and a quarter of each of the companies in the group. It is that assurance of working towards mutual benefit that keeps the group together sharing resources and contacts. We share certain administrative functions to save on costs, so we have a single company secretary, we defer all invoicing and receipts to headquarters and have a single bank location with individual accounts for each company. Gina is the only female acting managing director in the group, is virtually unknown by most and not particularly well respected by the rest of the companies and the main board is finely balanced between supporters and objectors.

It has taken me four months to persuade the board to appoint Gina to the main board and I have had to concede to allow a director appointed from the Tremblett & Son company to the board at the same time. Other than me, Gina will be pretty well on her own on The Tremblett Group board. Emotionally, she has been knocked sideways by the public shame of her husband's infidelity and her confidence as a woman able to hold onto a man has also taken a hammering."

"She is beautiful, Fred," I said, wanting to speak up for Gina, "and she's bright, comfortable in conversation, in fact quite playful, a joy to be with in company. And she certainly commands respect in her workplace."

"I think she feels confident in your presence, Harry, but that is because you act natural around her so she doesn't have to put on an act. Even though these are the mid-1970s, women are still rare in business, except in subordinate roles, and very rare indeed on company boards. She needs emotional and physical support, both after the day at home and at all the functions and work visits and negotiations that a board member is expected to attend and contribute to between meetings. We had considered using an actor to fill in as an escort on the public role, but they can be unreliable for a period which could extend from now until the new year or even the spring. All the actors we interviewed wanted to break up for the panto season."

I was amused at the thought of someone escorting Gina to the opera one night and playing Widow Twankey the next, and I told Fred so. Fred matched my mirth with a laugh and rueful grin.

"We are more concerned about the time after work and between functions, which a by-the-hour front man simply can't do. We're not just looking for someone who will keep her confidence up, comfort her when she has been hammered all day by people who know the job better than her, but a bit more than that," Fred smiled, "someone who cares enough to have a hankie ready and squeeze her hand when she needs it, like you did earlier, doing it without thinking. And as well as having empathy they need to be trustworthy enough not to take advantage of her when she's low. And somebody who is also careful enough not break her heart, or be fragile enough to have his own heart broken when the need to protect her has come to an end and Gina's priorities and perspectives diverge. So, Harry, are you that man?"

"Fred, your daughter is a beautiful woman and there is no doubt that any warm blooded man would give their eye teeth to have her as a wife or girlfriend, or just enjoy being in her orbit even it is all make-believe. As for Eric Tremblett's actions, if they are as bad as stated, well, words fail me. I was married for 19 years to my childhood sweetheart, and for me to imagine embarking on actions which would betray her trust was unthinkable. Mavis was put under different strains than I had to endure, a lot of pressure to bring up a family alone and suffer through loneliness for many years due to my weeklong absences for work. I thought I understood what she went through and tried to make up for it and even deluded myself that we had got past the worst of it and things would only get easier for us as the kids left the nest. I had to put up with loneliness on the road, and I put in long hours while away so that we could still have our weekends free. But Mavis abandoned me, she found comfort in another man, who she has since married. I cannot get my head around committing myself to another real relationship, even a temporary one, especially at my age. And, simply looking at what is around me, and particularly looking at Gina, I know that she is clearly way outside my league."

"It would only be temporary, Harry, a few months at best, half a year at worst. And you only have to play a role, not get involved emotionally.

But you never know what Gina may feel after a month or two. Eric was a much older man, and she fell in love with him, so don't count yourself out. Maybe she sees you in a different light to how you see yourself."

"Maybe the the age difference between Eric and Gina was what sparked his philandering, thinking that it was Gina who was losing her attraction to him?"

"No, I don't think so. Ever since the accident lots of girls, young women, and disgruntled husbands, have commented on his many affairs going all the way back. Even in possession of a pearl like Gina, Tremblett remained an absolute swine."

"Well, I think there's some eleven or twelve years age gap between us and that is a huge hurdle to jump. When I'm 65, tired and probably retired, Gina will still be in her early fifties, on her game and working at the height of her energetic powers, hopefully running this group of companies, preparing it for Giles to take over. But that's a long way into an impossible future, the fact now is that she is still a married woman and I hate those smooth talking seducers that prey on women who are either saddled with commitments, feel undervalued or are at a vulnerable point in their lives."

"So do I Harry, so do I. You know, I liked

Eric's father a lot, he was a good personal friend, probably my best friend, and he was a real gentleman. Eric took more after his flighty mother, who danced rings around my dear friend. Thank goodness I met, fell in love with and married Gina's mother and not someone who turned out like Eric's mother."

"I like Gina on a personal level and I would be happy to be able to regard her as a friend now and hopefully still in twenty years' time when all this malarky is just memories. And to do that I know I would have to be respectful of both her feelings and my emotions throughout this drama, so we can each come out of this intact at worst and enhanced in confidence at best. Then we can laugh about these few months in the future whenever we got together. I wouldn't play loose with women's feelings, especially people I like or who are a little fragile, like I think Gina is under the assured businesslike front she puts on, Fred. So, I can promise you that Gina will always be perfectly safe with me."

"I believe you, Harry my boy, so I'm right behind you in this. Right, the girls'll be back with us soon, so, are you ready for a dram or three of Blair Athol 13?"

"Yes, please, but I better have only the one, I do have to work tomorrow, and I am my own driver."

"Touché. I'll just make it a large one, then."

I had to smile at that. Gina's people, I thought then as I do now, were decent, down to earth, really nice genuine people. Basing myself here, escorting the lovely Gina for a couple of months, well, this wouldn't do me any harm, I thought, and it could be fun.

Later, back in the Gold Room, my room, really a small suite of bedroom and bathroom, I set my travel alarm clock to 7am. I set out my clothes ready for the morning as had become my habit.

After my second indulgent shower of the evening in that beautiful golden bathroom, I grabbed the folder from my slip case containing all the information on the companies I was due to visit that week and particularly reminded myself of the two appointments I had arranged across the very next morning.

I turned the bedside light off and settled down to sleep, but found I was tossing and turning reconciling myself to the task I had agreed to, of playing a role of escort over the next few months.

Was I up to it? Earlier that evening, with the support from Gina's parents, I had looked forward to it. Now, alone with my thoughts, I doubted it. Did I even want to do it? I surprised myself by an emphatic positive answer, yes.

Why did I want to do it? That was still a conflicting muddle and I always preferred order to muddle. I knew what my answer should be, as a gentleman of principle, in the spirit of altruism, but I was worried that my wanting to be around Gina and helping her was more in the Spirit of Ecstasy.

I had never been fazed by beautiful girls, but then I was never around them for long, a few moments in passing, part of a day at most before moving onto the next client; being constantly around Gina for several months, knowing my natural attraction to her, could I resist her? I would be foolish to think the age gap was a barrier to my feelings, however certain I was that it would be for her. I know she married an older man, but that was when she was a starry-eyed young woman in her teens, not the worldly-wise woman-once-scorned that she was now. She was a beautiful woman who I could be relaxed with if I knew I was meeting her fleetingly through business once a quarter, but seeing her, breathing her in and conversing with her daily, was another matter. Was I risking breaking my heart over the next few months?

Chapter 3
Tuesday 16 September 1975, 1.30 am

I was still lying awake when I heard a light knocking on my door.

"Harry, are you awake?" came the voice through the door.

I got up, switched on the bedside lamp, noticed the time was close to half past one, put on my dressing gown, walked to the door and twisted the huge antique key in the lock to unlock it. Gina stood there in the dark corridor, dressed in thick cotton pyjamas within an open dressing gown over her shoulders.

"Come in, Gina," I said softly, "how can I help you?"

"I can't sleep, Harry," she said apologetically, her head downcast. "Can you? If you could and did and I awoke you, then I'm sorry."

She seemed smaller, timid, hunched over and holding her hands together under her chin, as if begging, the opposite of how she portrayed herself at work, the restaurant and recently at dinner. She really was acting quite vulnerable right now, I thought.

"No," I smiled, "Like you, I've not slept a wink so far tonight, and I'm used to sleeping in strange beds."

"Do you think I could sleep with you ... here ... now, Harry?" she asked in a pleading tone, "I'll keep my PJs on, I just want the warm comfort and company of a friend."

"Then a friend you've found for the night," I nodded slowly. What harm could this be?

"We'll keep our pyjamas on, Gina, but you may inadvertently feel and therefore have to ignore my body's natural and unbidden reaction to your touch, heat and, no doubt, heavenly smell. I may possibly even react to any tiny sounds you make, like breathing for example," I chuckled and was rewarded by a slight smile. "But, as a friend, I will ignore my baser animal instincts and welcome you into a chaste but friendly embrace."

"You really lay down the house rules, eh? I feel like a girl in her first night in a boarding school," Gina giggled.

"We need rules if you are going to graduate top of the class, young lady," I growled as I held out my arms and she moved into them.

"Yes we do, thank you, headmaster," as she pushed her arms around my chest and tucked her head in just under my chin. My nose was almost buried in her hair and my senses were bombarded with the flowery smell of her shampoo, soap from her bath or shower and the unmistakable scent of a hot woman, her, the smell of Gina, absolutely intoxicating. For a man who had spent seven years without the touch of a woman or even one within a couple of yards of him without a table or desk between us, I felt overwhelmed and probably even more vulnerable than this woman I had pledged to protect and comfort!

"Which side of the bed did you sleep on with Mavis?" she asked, looking up at me.

"The right hand side, but that was only because it was nearest the door in our house and I was always first awake and up first in the morning."

"All right, I'll take the right side if I may. I used to sleep on the left and I felt that I wanted to change, to make this different, but I would defer to your preference."

"No, Gina, don't defer to me, please. Not all the time anyway. For the next couple of months, or however long this process takes, you must be more assertive in your private life as well as I know you are in your public one. Suggest what you think I might accept or order me to do something, expressed with good manners of 'please' and 'thank you', of course. I am strong willed enough to say 'No, because, etc, etc' if I object to your suggestion or order and we can then agree or negotiate an agreement between us as equals. It would serve to demonstrate to yourself that you are prepared to take charge, but also willing to change your position in light of reasoned argument or if you decide that your original stance was unimportant enough to you to agree to change to a different point of view. Decisive without overbearance, and remaining flexible where reason intervenes."

She regarded me with a smile playing on her lips. Then she pushed herself out of my arms, shucked the dressing gown off her shoulders and dived towards the bed, "Last one in bed turns out the light!"

Of course she beat me by miles, pulling the bed clothes up as far as her nose. I squeezed in beside her on the cold left hand side of the bed.

"Mmm, it's lovely and warm this side," she laughed, breathing in, "and it smells all manly and comforting."

"Gina, I'm going to have to lean over you from my side to turn out the light."

"I know," she said smugly.

"I'm going to have to almost climb all over you to reach that light."

"I still know," she giggled. "So, go on then, Harry, please climb over me."

I smiled, this was more like the Gina who

teased me walking round her dining room, not the timid waif standing at my bedroom door pleading for comfort a moment ago. I supported my upper body with my right elbow as I reached across to the lamp with my left hand. As my chest crossed her face, she reached up and bit me briefly through my pyjamas in the area of my left nipple.

"Ow!" I stopped, even moved away a little bit, so Gina clamped over my right nipple through my pyjamas and this time held on for a moment or two.

"Gina ... behave!" I said gently.

"Yes, headmaster, sorry, headmaster," she purred after releasing her jaws.

I switched out the light and settled back, "Are trying your hardest to get six of the best from me?"

Gina snuggled down, "I'm not even going to answer that, Harry, it's far too suggestive. Mmm, but just us doing this is nice and comfy, though, don't you think?"

"Yes, I do. Now, stop talking and go to sleep. I know I've got a lot to do tomorrow."

"So've I," Gina said, "it's my evening to visit Eric at the hospital tomorrow for a couple of hours. I know you said you'd come but this is rather short notice."

"Which hospital?"

"Reading General, on the west —"

"I know where it is, Gina, they have a small maintenance department that's in my patch, so I pop in every coupe of months. I'll drive you there and back home, and keep you company during your visit. I'd only be sitting in here working on my reports otherwise. I could catch up there, while you hold Eric's hand, or you could talk to us both about Trembletts and the individuals who you think we need to keep an eye on."

"Thank you, H, you're heaven sent."

"And you'd be an angel if only you stopped talking! You may not need it, but an old man like me needs all the beauty sleep going."

"Tosh! But I do feel relaxed enough to drop off now. So, night-night, H."

"Sweet dreams, Angel."

Chapter 4
Tuesday 16 September 1975, 5.30am

When I awoke with a short start, I found that I was spooning with Gina in a fetal position, both my arms wrapped around her, with one arm going dead with no feelings in it, the other palm resting on a warm, plump breast, my morning wood laying firmly like a log along the crack of her lovely bum.

It took me a couple of seconds to be fully aware of where I was and who I was with. She seemed to be breathing lightly and steadily and I breathed a shallow sigh of relief that she was still asleep.

My arm that was resting on her breast had her arm resting on it, so very slowly I straightened out my legs, then rolled away from her, pulling my hand away from her breast and under her arm.

However, I could do little about my buried arm, although the slight movements I had just made started off a bout of excruciating 'pins and needles' as the blood started to reflow and my nerve ends started to wake up and let me know that they hurt like bloody hell.

Gina snuffled a tiny moan at my movement, but didn't appear to waken. I shuffled my bum away from her, then turned back towards her and lifted my upper torso, leaving me room to pull out my dead arm. I did that quickly in one movement, then rolled away so my back was towards her. My released arm was now a paroxysm of pain as every nerve ending signalled its displeasure of rude awakening, and I flexed the arm, wrist and fingers to speed up the process.

Gina woke, her breathing pattern shortened and was shallower. I pretended to breathe slowly and deeply, though my heart was racing like a Husqvana on a steep and slippery hill climb. Gina sighed and moved, rolling onto her back, so her shoulder touched my back and her arm that had previously cuddled me to her breast, explored the space between us and settled on the upper cheek of my bum.

"Harry?" Gina enquired softly, tentatively, "You awake?"

"I'm awake, Gina. Did you sleep well?" I asked as I turned, my arm still half asleep and felt hot and heavy, like a yule log smouldering internally.

"Yes, I slept like a log, thank you, H. While

this is lovely, though, I really must get up, before we're discovered."

As she threw the covers off her and scrambled out her side of the bed, she said, "Don't forget, you're taking me to work this morning, I like to leave about twenty to eight?"

"No problem."

"Well, have a lay-in for another hour, it's only five-thirty. See you later." And she was out of the door and gone.

I turned back and rolled myself into the warm area she had just vacated. I luxuriated in her smell that clung to the sheets and pillow and lay there until the intensity of her presence faded. I showered and dressed, repacked my papers in my slim briefcase and took the back stairs down to the kitchen.

"Good morning Linda, Tom," I greeted the couple who were sitting at the kitchen table drinking tea.

"How well did you sleep, Mr Harry?" Linda asked with a knowing smile as she rose up out of her seat and waving me to sit, "Bed not too ... lumpy was it?"

"No, I slept really well, a litle while after I settled and the bed was absolutely perfect. And, please, just call me Harry." I wondered how on Earth it was possible to keep secrets in a well-established household, where probably every creaking floorboard in every corridor was known to those who'd lived here longest.

"Tea or coffee, Harry?"

"Tea please."

"I'll pour it," Tom said from the table, "come and take the weight off," as he turned an upturned cup in a saucer, "milk?"

"Please."

"Sugar?"

"Yes, two, please," I sat myself down on a spare chair at the table.

"What do you want for breakfast?" Linda asked, "we've got various cereals or porridge to start with, grilled bacon, eggs how you want them, toast, black pudding, sausages, beans, tomatoes, mushrooms, and toast."

"I'll have some cornflakes, then bacon, poached or scrambled egg, and a round of toast, please."

"Young Tom took the liberty of taking your keys and parking the Rolls-Royce in the garages at the back." Tom said, "while you were dining last night. He's washed and polished it ready for you today. Tonight you can park it in that same space in the garage, the combination lock on the garage door is 3971. Hope you don't mind?" He put my keys on the table.

"Not at all, but I prefer to be asked," I said quietly, "I'm very protective of my car."

"Of course, it is a beautiful motor," Tom said, bowing his head slightly. "I would have asked but it had just started to rain and by then you were in the library conversing with Mr King and he doesn't like to be disturbed."

"Yes, and I am not used to drinking so much whisky before a working day, I'm looking forward to a dry night tonight."

"Mrs Tremblett has informed us that you will be dining at five sharp tonight, Harry," Linda said as she set down a glass of fresh orange before him, "Thank you for driving her to the hospital, she often returns quite upset from those visits and we fear for her on those roads late at night."

"She'll be perfectly safe with me, Linda."

Both the servants smiled. "We know," they chorused.

𝕽

Gina explained the week's itinerary, "Tonight and Thursday evenings I will be visiting Eric —"

"We ... will be visiting Eric, both nights."

"Yes, thank you, Harry, both nights. On Wednesday evening, well, late afternoon really, we have to drive to London for the weekly

Tremblett Group board meeting in head office in Mayfair. Daddy tells me that we need to leave here between three o'clock and three thirty," she looked at me from the passenger seat, "if you could...."

"I could. Just go through your itinerary. The only cast iron dates coming up is next Tuesday and the following Saturday when I need to go back to Brum."

"What for?"

"We are playing local derbies against Wolves and Birmingham City. I would hate to miss those two games."

"All right," Gina consulted her list, "I can make both of those dates, by moving Eric's visit to Monday that week."

"Gina, I don't have access to an executive box for those games, I'm just a season ticket holder of a single numbered seat in the stand for our home game and I have bought a standing room only ticket in the terraces for the away match. There probably won't be any more tickets available this late in the day, as both grounds will be filled to capacity. They always are for local derbies."

"I'll phone Daddy and see what he can arrange. He knows a lot of people, including friends in Birmingham. You are offering to attend my events, so I want to attend yours.

It's only fair and I know that I will enjoy the experience with you. I love the excitement of live sport."

I chuckled. Gina was unlike any other woman I knew.

"Now, on Friday, most of the King's office staff and supervisers go down to *The Four Horseshoes* in town for a drink after work. Some of the staff are in constant contact with Head Office and, seeing us together, and knowing that we have only just met, will definitely get back to head office on the gossip telegraph quicker than it being on the front page of the *Daily Mail.* Then, on Sunday afternoon there will be a garden party fundraiser for the local Conservative Party and our MP will be there along with most of the businesses in the constituency, so you may pick up some useful contacts. Next Monday we could visit Eric, leaving us free to drive up to Birmingham on Tuesday afternoon."

"If we go up to Brum early afternoon, I can call into the offices and get my paperwork filed and pick up my files for next week. I was going to cover the Bristol area next week, but will do Reading and Slough instead so I'm close by and handy."

I dropped Gina off at work, leaving her the telephone numbers of the offices I was due to visit that day, then drove off to Tewksbury followed by Gloucester, which were follow up visits to existing customers to check how they were doing and having a nose around to look for any potential opportunities to cold call on. When I arrived at my second appointment, the Receptionist passed me a message to call Gina.

"King & Son, how can I help you?"

"Good morning, it's Harry Crab —"

"Hello, Harry, I'll pass you straight through to Gina, hold on."

"Thanks Polly." I waited a moment, glancing at the Gloucester Receptionist in front of me, who smiled at me, knowing I was waiting to be connected.

"Would you like a coffee, Harry?" she whispered.

"Ooh, please, black, two sugars."

She nodded, "I'll tell Mr Brown you're here when you've finished your call."

"Thanks, Denise — Oh, hello, Gina, it's Harry, you wanted —?"

"Yes, H, got a couple of things for you," she said. "Are you still in Gloucester this afternoon?"

"Yes, I was going to cold call into two or three places, no set appointments yet."

"You've got one appointment now, at 2 o'clock, Mr Tomlinson at Rawlings & Smith, do you know where they are?"

"Bloody hell, yes, been trying to get in there

for years but can't make any headway, Tomlinson their buyer wants some significant greasing just to get an appointment and I'm not prepared to play any of his games."

"Well, the instruction to see you has come directly from the boardroom. Daddy knows them well from when he was chairman of the trade association they belong to. Greasing? What does that mean?"

"Backhanders, greasing palms, if you don't give Tomlinson what he wants on the side you've no chance of a contract ... he's notorious, not paid for a stick of furniture or white goods in his house, nor paid for a holiday since his in-laws paid for his honeymoon twenty years ago. Normally, I'd hate to have to deal with him, but if I can just get in to see him without paying for it, that would be a treat in itself, just to see him squirm. And if I do get a chance to quote for what they need, I could always post it to the member of the board your father knows instead and blame the transmission on a clerical error at our end."

"So he's notorious for it, is he, this greasing, and not just for the supply of nuts and bolts?"

"No, he buys everything that Rawlings needs. They make electric motors, milk floats, motorised bicycles, mobility wheelchairs, etc and I've heard from a reliable source that his wife's new car was paid for by the company Rawlings get all their heavy-duty batteries from."

"Interesting. You'll have to let me know how you get on later tonight. Oh, and you can resell your Wolverhampton Wanderers stand ticket as we both have invitations to the VIP lounge as personal guests of a Mr Stan Cullis. And we also have invitations to the VIP box at Villa Park for the Birmingham City match as guests of a Mr Pat Matthews."

"Wow! Your Dad has been busy. Tell him I really do appreciate it."

"I think that he's just been having fun, Harry, enjoying himself by contacting old friends and calling in a few favours."

When I reached Rawlings & Smith that afternoon, I introduced myself and told the Receptionist that I had an appointment with Mr Tomlinson.

I was informed with a sly smile from the Receptionist that I was indeed expected but that Mr Tomlinson was no longer with the company and that Mr Edmunds, a senior director, was seeing me instead.

"When did Mr Tomlinson leave?" I asked after she had informed Mr Edmunds' secretary at the other end of the line of my arrival.

"About an hour ago, he left in high dungeon," she whispered.

I smiled at her common mistake of 'dudgeon'.

"Unexpected was it?" I whispered back.

"Came in this morning, he did, his usual half-hour late but before the MD comes in, full of hisself as usual and three hours later most of the board of directors turned up out of the blue for a special meeting. Mr T was called to the board room and next we see he's been escorted out the door with all his personals in a small cardboard box."

"Sorry to see him go?"

"No, not at all," she whispered, looking around to check the Reception area was empty. "Thomlinson was not well liked, too haughty for words, like he was always smirking as he checked to see if my blouse was transparent. Fair gave me the shivers, he did."

I smiled, "Sounds like his unexpected marching orders couldn't have happened to a nicer bloke."

She giggled back, "Yeah, that's what we've all been saying."

Just than a secretary rushed through the door and urged that I follow her up to the offices.

I turned to the Receptionist and bade her an interesting rest of the day, and she wished me the best of luck with a beaming smile.

I was ushered into a comfortable office, dark wood-lined in oak, with old pictures of the

Victorian founders of the ancient company and pictures of old steam engines and a factory floor with pulleys and overhead leather belts driving the old machinery a hundred or more years ago. Sitting at a heavy and ancient desk was a tall, older and distinguished-looking man with a grey moustache, who stood up smiling, walked around the desk with hand outstretched and grabbed my hand firmly. My first thought was that his picture wouldn't look at all out of place alongside those fine Victorian gentlemen.

"Stan Edmunds, Harry, glad to make your acquaintance. I suppose you heard from Amanda the dramatic to-do we've had early this afternoon?"

"Er..."

Stan laughed, "Don't worry, Amanda's an inveterate gossip, which is sometimes used to our advantage. For one thing, it meant that you had a chance to absorb the idea of Tomlinson going before you got up here."

"Yes, I assumed he had been caught out and, well, I suspect that Fred King has been speaking to you?"

"He has, and on his tip-off we've had our finance director climbing all over it. Naturally, you, Harry, have only just heard about it for the first time from Amanda, so no blame for any tip-off will remotely gravitate in your direction."

"I appreciate the thinking behind that thought, Mr Edmunds."

"Right, first things first, what's your poison? And if you're going to hesitate joining me, let me tell you that what we've discovered and had to deal with today I need a really stiff one myself and was only holding off indulging by awaiting your arrival."

"I'm hospital visiting tonight with a lovely young lady, so I don't want to drink too much, or have the smell of drink on my breath. But I don't mind sharing a moderate dram of malt whisky with a drop of water with you, Mr Edmunds."

"Good man, call me Stan, everybody else up here in the gods of the company does. Park yourself in one of the armchairs." He busied himself with the drinks while I seated himself. Stan brought the drinks over and we exchanged cheers, clinking glasses together.

"You helped us a lot with getting rid of a cancer in our midst. We were aware of the odd Christmas box but had no idea of the full extent of his corruption. I won't tell you how we managed it of course, but within the hour we had faxes of his bank statements, deposit accounts, *et cetera*, now all frozen by his bank until we release them. We didn't wait for the courts to freeze his accounts, but the bank is cooperating fully with us but will deny any involvement if challenged. After we told Tomlinson what we had on him, he had to write us a substantial cheque in compensation before we let him leave here without calling in the police to escort him. We will unfreeze his deposit accounts, transfer the balances to his current and restore the funds to our coffers before we unfreeze his current accounts."

"It's refreshing to see justice served, Stan, so cheers agsin!"

"Cheers to you again, nHarry. Now, down to business. Would you care to take a look at this list?"

Stan picked up one of two sheets of foolscap lying on the coffee table by the armchairs.

"This is a list of fixings, nuts and bolts and self-tapping screws that we mostly use, along with the quantities we need urgently, which equates to about a normal month's supply. Would you be able to give us some ball park prices on these this afternoon and an idea when you could deliver these quantities soonest?"

He handed the list of about twenty items.

"And," he added, "then let us know what your normal price for regularly monthly supplies would be for these quantities?"

I looked down the list of 22 numbered items quickly but carefully, taking into account the quantities required for each. With one or two exceptions, they were mostly listed in order of usage, with larger numbers at the top and lower at the bottom.

"This item 21 near the bottom, we don't have much demand if any for these in Class 2A 70 stainless steel, so I know we won't have any stock. I will ring the office and get an idea of the chances of producing some by the end of the week. Items 1 to 10 I would guess we could supply all but two or three of them in this quantity by the Friday, the exceptions we could get you at least half by Friday and the balance early next week. All the other items listed you could definitely have those kind of quantities this week."

As I took a slim notebook out of my pocket, along with a 'screws ready reckoner' booklet, Stan nodded with a smile that he understood the estimation and my confidence in the supply. I quickly jotted down a list of figures on the foolscap from top to bottom, after referring to my notebook, then I used the ready reckoner to write down a second set next to the first set of figures until I finished and handed the sheet back to Stan. The exercise took no more than about three or four minutes.

"The first row of figures is my company's basic price per thousand of each of these items, the second figure is the price we would offer them per thousand at the monthly quantities you require them, including the first delivery. This discount ranges from 10% across the larger items, down to 2% at the bottom, although those prices are more based on the overall level of supply rather than if you only opt to buy those individual items. Look over those figures and compare with what you have on your list and I'll speak to my office about getting you the supplies delivered from stock and getting these stainless steel bolts into production."

"I understand, Harry. Use the phone at the desk, just dial '9' for an outside line, wait for the tone and dial your number. I'm going to call in our accounting manager, she's more adept on the calculator than I am and the prices I've got on my copy of the list here are what we pay for each month's quantity. But do go ahead on making those stainless steel bolts, if nothing else we'll readily pay whatever it costs for those. What I will tell you is that we have told the current suppliers that Tomlinson has admitted he took bribes from them for years and we would have expected them through professional curtesy to have been informed about this criminal activity at least at Director level. They've been told that, as they are all in clear breach of our contracts, that they will collect every single item they supplied that we still hold in stock and they will reimburse us what we paid for them within seven days, or we will announce this turn of events and the newsworthy reasons behind it to the press and general public. They will be collected on Friday and they have already delivered a banker's draft with the signatures still wet, to repay us for every nut and bolt we have estimated we hold in stock. We took the opportunity to return all the non-metric stock which we no longer use, on the basis that they supplied that stock while they were bribing our employee and charging us inflated prices."

I had to smile, "I'm sorry that casual remark, made in exasperation to Fred's daughter, has caused you so much upheaval."

Stan said with a grin, "Well, it's going to be interesting around here for a while as we adjust to better ways of working, Harry, and you don't need to apologise to me for a thing."

I rang my office, okayed the stainless steel job in principle initially with the sales director, who was delighted to have any inroad at all into Rawlings & Smith, knowing what a hard nut it had been to crack.

Then I was put through to the production manager, Bob Andrews, who I have always had a great relationship with. I explained the material and size specification of the nuts and bolts, with the quantities needed on a monthly basis, and I was assured that he could get the raw material in overnight and start production late Wednesday or early Thursday and may even manage to produce the required quantity during overtime on the Thursday night. The production manager would check out the order for all the rest of the supplies when it came through over the fax and confirm delivery first thing Friday morning. When I told him about the two or three items I had supply concerns about, he told me to leave it with him, saying he wouldn't led me down if he could help it.

By the time I concluded his call, Stan had a woman with him using a calculator to work through the figures, her fingers flying across the keys. I hung back waiting for them to finish while savouring that small glass of malt whisky, deep in the offices of a company I had never dreamed of selling to.

Soon they were finished entering figures and continued to converse in whispers as they compared their figures on their sheet with the ones on my sheet. Occasionally the woman would point to a figure than make a fresh calculation on her machine. Then she sat back primly, with her knees together and rested her hands with the calculator on her lap. She smiled at me, quite a nice, shy smile, Harry thought; she was in her late forties, had no rings on her fingers, wore no make up that he could see, and her mousey hair was tied up in a tight bun.

When Stan had finished looking through the figures, he dismissed her with thanks, and she got up and walked out.

"Come sit down here, Harry, what did your production chap say about Friday?"

"You'll pretty well get most of item 21 by first thing Friday. He's getting back to me regarding all the rest, but I am sure he'll have little trouble in getting most of the other items on the same delivery if I can confirm the order by tomorrow at noon."

"You can order them now, Harry, in these quantities set out and assume similar quantities every calendar month from now on. Other than two items, your basic price beats the prices we've been paying, and those you didn't were only half and just over one percent lower than your basic price, without taking into account the ten percent discount you are offering on the major items. Is there any delivery charge or rush order charge on the stainless steel?"

"No, regular deliveries by our vans is included in our overheads, and those nuts and bolts will be on that regular delivery. Otherwise, a rush order sent by an overnight courier or unscheduled van would be extra but you would be advised of the cost of that at the time of placing the order. I'll get the office to firm up on the figures, once I fax my sheet over to them, they won't change by any more than a percent either way. In fact I am happy to sign that as a contract here and now."

"No need for that, Harry, here, let's shake on it as gentlemen that the contract will be around the kind of area we have discussed." We shook on it.

"On that contract when you get it," I said, as we finished our drinks, "will be set out the prices and at what quantities the various discounts kick in, a list of contact names and telephone numbers, so your staff can call direct to sales, production, accounts and speak to your on the road contacts at any time. There will also be set out our expected delivery date times, which we will fit in with other deliveries to the area, and the latest time you may adjust the order for that delivery, either by phone or fax. Once your chaps have done it a couple of times, they'll find the ordering system is really simple to use. If you want, we could divide the quantities by four and deliver weekly, but still invoice through a monthly statement. And I would recommend that in a couple of weeks you consider ordering enough stock for about three months, which would ensure you never run out even if you get the unexpected spike in the production process."

"Sound advice, we'll let the production managers sort that out between them, Harry."

"Call my office if you need me, otherwise I generally look in at regular intervals to check everything is going OK. I like to check direct with the shop floor guys, too, as they are the ones most concerned about how supplies are packaged or presented, to ensure a smooth transition between suppliers. That way we hone best practice so that we deliver the best service. No point in just keeping management happy if the guys using the supplies are having problems or have great suggestions to make which will improve what we can do for you."

"So, you were a production chap once?" Stan smiled.

"Yes, indentured and fully qualified engineer."

"Me too," said Stan, "and mostly I miss it, but not today, I've loved today, making good decisions and establishing a great partnership. This is a great result for our company. Now, be off with you, Harry, you've a lovely young lady to escort tonight."

"I do indeed, I'm off."

The hospital room was bright, too bright for the unenviable atmosphere of a dying man hanging onto life by a hopeless thread, I thought. The body of a man, with only his pale almost cod-fish white face on show, dominated the focus of the room. His skin had an oily sheen to it, paper thin and stretched over shallow cheeks with all the veins showing through, giving a slightly blue tint to his palette. His nose and mouth was covered with a breathing mask and the expanding and contracting squeeze box, which dictated the rise and fall of the chest, on a trolley at the side of the bed, was making the only noise in the room. His hair and eyebrows were perfectly white. His arms, laying outside the thin sheets covering his unmoving body, were injected with drips feeding in saline and presumably nutrients as he was obviously 'nil by mouth'.

Gina sat down in the chair next to the bed and spoke to the body with a cheery and chatty tone, "Good evening, Eric, it's Gina. I'm visiting you with a friend of mine called Harry Crabtree, he is one of King & Son's suppliers." She looked up at me expectantly.

"Hello, Eric, it's a pleasure to meet you," I responded.

"We are going to be talking about Trembletts, Eric," Gina explained to the near-corpse. "We have a board meeting tomorrow to confirm me temporarily filling a place on the board while you are incapacitated. As you know from an earlier conversation, my father stepped up to fill the Chairman's role and your cousin Jack Collins became Deputy. Harry here is lending me some moral support when I make my pitch for membership. Obviously I'll be briefed by Daddy on what to say and keep the board looking forward to expanding the group in the next twelve months. Everything is ticking over nicely, under Dad's leadership, but some of the companies in the group are having problems with inflation, the rising cost of fuel and energy prices, and increasing wage demands from workers. Trembletts & Co are already considering cutting the work force by 10%, in the light of wage demands of 27%."

Gina whispered to me, as I had found a chair in the corridor and had just sat down next to her, "No reaction to that at all, if there was something going on in his head, you'd think he'd react to that?"

"Are those figures right?" I asked quietly.

"Trembletts is the core business in the group, but is poorly run compared with other companies in the group, but I did exaggerate slightly, they are considering 8% redundancies in light of union wage demands of 25%, while the office and other non-union staff have already settled for 15%. The group took a big hit during the Government-imposed Three Day Week last year, when the electric power was cut off two days every week. However, we made diesel generators within the group that enabled us to mostly stay open, as well as increased our sales of generators. This increased our overheads but maintained our production and market share. This year we have seen most of our companies enjoy an upturn. However, these are still worrying times for us, for the Labour Government, and for the country, but the short term forecast is improving month by month."

"All right, tell me about the board meeting tomorrow."

"With Eric stuck in here and no longer in control, the group board has been one director short for four months. Dad was deputy chairman so he automatically took the chair. When it almost immediately looked like Eric wouldn't be returning to work, Dad proposed that I join the board through a co-option until formally elected at the AGM by the shareholders, but he failed to win a majority vote. Trembletts have never had a female board member before and the dinosaurs are fighting a rearguard action. Another month went by and Dad tried again, this time the other directors proposed their own champion, a non-executive Director from Trembletts & Co, and the vote ended in a dead heat, so Dad proposed that me and the Trembletts' candidate both attend this meeting, give a short presentation and vote again, to have one or other or both join the board."

"And you have already prepared your presentation?"

"Yes, I can run through it with you tonight if you like," she said and, after I nodded, continued, "Thank you."

Her presentation was a single sheet of quarto folded in her handbag.

I asked some relevant questions and made just a couple of suggestions at the end of her presentation rehearsal, falling back on my many years as a salesman, often having to pitch myself and my company as a fresh idea to buyers who were otherwise happy to leave current arrangements well alone.

During our conversation, in which Gina addressed updates to the comatose Eric, I discovered that The Tremblett Group was made up of 15 companies, although three of them were wholly owned subsidiaries of Tremblett & Co, so the main board was made up of twelve non-executive directors, one from each main company, plus the chairman, finance director, sales director and the sixteenth member, who was the company secretary to all the companies, a lawyer by trade.

The issue about Gina's membership was because Fred had stepped up to be acting chairman, and he wanted Gina to replace Fred as representing King & Son; the amendment to the proposal which was passed by a narrow majority of the board was that if Gina was coming on board, Tremblett & Co should have a second representation to replace Eric's vote on the board. Fred had no choice to break the deadlock but to agree and the two candidates had to make presentations and be officially voted on, even though the board had already agreed in principle to the appointments.

Gina then ran through some of the details of the directors she knew from dealings with head office. She was going to be the first ever female member of the group board.

The new temporary deputy chairman was naturally the current representative from Tremblett & Co, one of Eric's cousins that even Eric didn't like, Jack Collins, who was also an insurance broker.

There were several members of the Collins clan on the board of Tremblett & Co, including a nasty set of twins, that Gina had met at various group meetings and parties, although they were not on the main board. The finance director was

Sam Elliott, who Gina thought was honest and had a dry sense of humour; she was certain that she could persuade Sam that purchase orders to my company could have King & Son's address on, even though the payments would still go through head office, so that I could be credited with the sale.

I reminded Gina that that really wasn't necessary, I could and would still service the account, but she flashed her eyes and was adamant.

The sales director was an odd fish, an Alec Johns, an ex military man, who mainly seemed to spend his time having lunches, as the holding company really didn't sell anything, just provided centralised services.

Gina agreed that one of her tasks once she became chairman on the board was going to be investigating the individual businesses in the group and weeding out the many make-weights that were in key positions.

After two hours of non-stop talking, directing most of the information for my benefit at the silent, unmoving body next to us, continually punctuated by the incessant menchenical racket from the breathing machine, we had both had enough for one night.

On the drive home of just over twenty miles through a cold rainy night, which at that time of night took about thirty-five minutes, I decided to talk about other subjects that a supposed couple should know.

"So tell me, Gina, what do you like to do in your spare time, when you are not working?"

"Oh, I busy myself shopping for clothes, particularly for Giles as he is shooting up like a weed on pep pills." Gina replied, "I shop for presents, not only for me to give, but I used to buy all the presents that Eric and Giles gave out at Christmas, birthdays and anniversaries, too. To relax I like to read in the evenings with my feet up. Occasionally I go out with some old university friends for a meal and drinks, but then only a couple of times a year."

"I could massage your feet while you're reading," I said, which made her smile, "What do you do at weekends?"

"I used to catch up with the washing and ironing, but at home with my parents they have Linda to take care of most of that. I didn't have as much help at home, just a woman that came in for an hour a day to do some dust and hoover cleaning. I don't even have to cook and I used to enjoy cooking when Giles was home."

"When did Giles go off to school?"

"When he was seven. There was a little prep school that was fairly local at first, but now he is at a boarding school in Surrey. They don't like us to visit too often, says it spoils their sense of independence apparently, but he comes home between terms for two or three weeks, with eight weeks in July and August, plus I visit him two Sundays each term."

"What do you do on your visits?"

"Giles shows me his room and what work he has been doing." Gina smiled as she spoke, I took my eye off the road for a moment to see. "Every time he goes up a year he shows me around the classrooms he is working in, all the mums and dads do that. Samples of their work adorn the walls and he proudly shows me any of his pieces on display. We might stroll around the beautiful grounds there, depending on the weather. Then I take him out for a lunch, we walk around the nearby town and stock him up with sweets and stuff to last a couple of weeks, then we have an afternoon tea before we take him back in time for their supper and cocoa."

"When are you due to visit him again?"

"Three weeks' time. Would you like to come? I would love to introduce you and it would give us a chance to do the whole school tour again."

"Of course, if you don't think Giles would be upset —"

"No, of course not, Eric hardly ever came on my visits, he wasn't good father material, but I didn't know that when we married. I'll write and tell Giles in advance, so if he feels it would be embarrassing to be driven out to lunch in a sparkling Rolls-Royce...."

"All right. Now, you've told me what you actually do in your spare time, but what would you really like to do, what would you like to learn more about, or, what is it that you would like to do but never really had the opportunity to try before?"

Gina was quiet for a while.

"Come on, Gina, there must be a wish list somewhere in your head?"

"Right, Harry. I used to love dancing, but don't get a chance to do it any more. I love to sing and always wanted to sing in a band, so I would love to take up singing lessons. My brother is a sailor and when we were children my father had a small sailing boat on a lake that we all used to go out sailing in. I would like to do some of that again. And horse riding, we never kept horses here but I used to have a pony at a riding school as a girl and would love to take that up again."

"All right, you've set me a challenge to organise all or some of these activities in the next few weeks."

"Really?"

"Yes, Gina, I am not having you sitting and moping at home, like a grieving widow or a disappointed divorcee. You are going to get out and be active as if you are young, vibrant and alive to new experiences. Honestly, you'll sleep better and, with your blood racing you will stop being depressed and start to live your life again as you should."

"You think I am depressed, Harry?"

"Yes I do, and it takes one to know one. I was devastated when my marriage ended. My confidence was shot to pieces, all my energy drained away and I started staying in and ignoring the world. You know that I am a people person, but during those first couple of years I would go months without talking to anyone other than through my job. The Roller, when she found me and made me buy her, made a big difference to how I regarded myself and my value."

"How?"

"People started to talk to me, well really they just wanted to talk about the car. So I was forced to talk to people and soon I looked forward to taking the car to places where I would met people and feel that I really was part of the world again."

"Yes, I suppose I have shut myself off, not all the time, but yes, I really have started the process to shut down."

"Well, now's the time to rev up your engine,

Gina, my love, and live. And I'm just the man to encourage you or do it!"

ℝℝ

I left the bedroom door unlocked and ajar that Tuesday night, with one of the bedside lamps left on when I retired. I was pleasantly dozing when I heard the click of the door closing. I turned over, she was standing at what used to be her side of the bed shivering. It was a lovely house, but a cold one that needed constant fires burning to keep warm.

"You're on my side," she observed.

"I know, I'm just warming it up for you. I'll shift over," which I did, to about halfway across the bed. She turned the light out, slipped in and snuggled up to me.

"Ooh, you're lovely and warm, H," Gina mumbled, her lips pressed vibrating against my chest.

Without thinking, I gently kissed the top of her head and said, "You're lovely".

She squeezed up to me, laying on her side, put her head on my shoulder, undid one of the middle buttons of my pyjama top and slipped her cold hand in to warm it up against my furry chest. I pulled the covers over her up to her chin while my other arm wrapped around her and stroked her back and shoulder.

"Ow, your feet and hands are cold!" I complained, as one icy foot insinuated between my knees and the other rested on my warm feet, warming her freezing sole.

"And your toe nails need cutting," Gina protested, her cold foot wriggling and wrestling with my warm ones to get warm on both top and bottom.

"You offering?"

"Mmm, I used to cut Giles' toenails when he was little and at home. He was always creeping into my bed of a morning at weekends, and his feet were like ten tiny daggers. He doesn't do that any more since the school made him more independent. Have a long hot soak in the bath after we finish work early tomorrow and before lunch. I'll cut your toe nails for you while they're nice and soft, I've got a little travel bag full of neat pedicure stuff."

"So long as you don't paint them vivid colours, I'll be happy."

"Spoilsport! I wouldn't have to put on a fake smile during my presentation at the board meeting tomorrow, if all I had to do was think of you, all manly and serious, standing tall and strong, supporting me in my hour of need like a hero, knowing all the time that you were wearing shiny bright red nails under your sensible man shoes and socks!" she giggled.

"Tut tut! The things I am required to do in your service, Ma'am."

"You are too good to me, H," she sighed and snuggled even closer.

Soon she was asleep, but I was awake a long time listening to her breathe in and out and feeling the heat of her voluptuous body next to me, laying relaxed and trusting in my arms.

Being an uninvolved escort was becoming a challenge.

Chapter 5
Wednesday 17 September 1975, 1.30pm

I picked Gina up from the office just after working through lunchtime, so we could shower or bathe and change for the important board meeting in London.

I eased the car through the heavy afternoon London traffic, with Gina sitting up front next to me. When we got close to head office, set in a large steel and glass building, I stopped at the side of the road for a moment and Gina transferred to the back seat.

For this occasion, I thought it was best to just be her driver. We walked in, with me walking respectfully just behind her, carrying her slim brief case.

The ante room to the board room was a comfortable lounge with wingback chairs grouped around tables and a fully fitted cocktail bar in the corner of the room with a couple of bar stools next to it. The board members were standing around in groups of three or four, making small talk. Weaving in and around them, two young and attractive cocktail waitresses, dressed in short tight black dresses with frilly white aprons and lace head caps, were holding out trays of drinks and canapés, a choice of orange juice or champagne in the glasses.

No wonder, I thought, these old board directors didn't give proper respect to potential female board members.

Fred came over and welcomed his daughter's arrival with a warm hug.

Before he could shake my hand I handed her the slip case, slightly bowing as I did so, and reverted to my childhood Brummie accent.

"Oy'll wait in the corner for yow, ma'am," I said, nodded silently to Fred and retreated backwards a respectable step or two before I turned and walked over to the bar, where an attractive young woman behind the bar offered me a drink with a sweet red-lipped smile.

"Just a tonic water, please, Oy'm drivin'," I said.

I had worked in the south west of England five days out of seven for almost 25 years, with most of my clients speaking what is politely known as the Queen's English, so my natural West Midlands' dialect, centred around the Brummie accent, was reduced to just a hint as a natural part of my everyday speech, which I couldn't quite shake off even if I wanted to.

Today, pretending to be Gina's driver, I

decided to speak as though I had just got off the bus, or 'booz' in Brum.

I turned and watched as about half the board members also turned and welcomed Gina, who was looking stunning in a modest but well-cut navy blue business suit, the hem fashionably just above the knee, while the other half of the room looked down their noses at her. Other than the waitresses, Gina was the only female present in the room.

At a signal that Harry didn't see, they all put their glasses down and retired into the boardroom, leaving Gina and a tall, dapper looking gentleman behind, as the serving girls took their cue and disappeared. The man gravitated towards Gina and engaged her in a brief conversation.

From her body language, Harry saw that the conversation, or even the presence of the man, who Harry guessed was in his early forties, was unwelcome. He had invaded her space, so she half turned, taking one step back, turning into partly seeing me in at least her periphery vision.

I saw her tiny smile form on her lips, like Mona Lisa, and just knew she was remembering the fun we had had earlier while she did what felt like a professional pedicure on my feet. I hadn't minded at all because the whole process had got us giggling like happy children, but I did have the thought flash across my mind that if I had a traffic accident on the way home and ended up in a side ward like poor Eric Tremblett, how seriously would the medical profession regard me and my bright red shiny toe nails?

The board room door opened and Gina was ushered in to give her five minute presentation. I knew she was confident in what she had to say because we had gone through it several times and I felt she'd be word perfect.

The man she had briefly conversed with walked over to the bar and perched on the only other bar stool as he ordered a large pink gin, which the girl behind the bar prepared for him, then she left to collect up the used glasses left lying around by the departed board members.

"So," he addressed me between sips of his drink, "I understand that you're Gina Tremblett's driver?"

"Oy am, yow know. Harry's my name." I held out my hand. The man took it reluctantly and shook it limply.

"I'm Rupert, Rupert Bambridge, I'm up for a place on the board and have to give my presentation when she's finished. She's married to my boss, Eric Tremblett, d'you know him?"

I shook my head without saying anything.

"He's a bit banged up in hospital apparently. So, what's Mrs Tremblett like to work for, I mean what's it like having to take orders from a woman, eh?"

"Well, Oy spent all my early years tekin' orders from moi Moom, so Oy have no trouble tekin' instruction from Mrs Tremblett, although she usually asks me to do things rather than orderin' me, it makes a difference, yow know. She's been super so far, but then Oy've only bin workin' for her for three days. I started on Moondee about lunchtoyme. But she's very bin very friendlay towards me so far."

"She's gorgeous too isn't she, what? I'd like to get my hands on her, I'm a tits and arse man myself and, man, she's got both them in spades."

"Look myte, yow're talkin' about ma boss and Oy don't loike yow attitude. She should at least expect respect from the loikes o' yow."

"Of course, of course, don't mind me old chap, just a bit nervous, got to give a jolly old speech in a minute, you know?"

"I wouldn't worry myte, Mrs Tremblett said yow both were certain shoe-ins for the board already."

"Quite, quite, well, we'll see, what. I'm ready for another snifter, though, how about you?"

"Oy'm driving, so Oy'm stickin' to a bottle o' pop, an' this one'll see me owt."

"Another large pink gin, please girl," he ordered the girl who had just come back from collecting the used glasses from the tables. In the time it took her to put the tray of dirty glasses down safely and collect a fresh glass, he impatiently said, "Come on girl, one doesn't have all night, you know!"

The girl, 'Mary' according to her name tag, swirled a couple of ice cubes around a fresh glass, ensuring the inside was evenly coated in a thin film of ice cold water, tossed out the ice back into the bucket, shook and unscrewed a bottle and dropped two drops of angostura bitters into the glass, and screwed up the bottle again, and returned it to its place on the shelf. Then she swirled the bitters around the glass with a practiced flick of the wrist before pouring two measures of Beefeater gin from an overhead optic. She handed it to Rupert who tossed the contents of the carefully prepared glass down in one.

Just then the door to the boardroom opened and Gina emerged. She walked over and told Rupert they were ready for him and he dashed off.

"I'm dying for the loo," Gina said after he left, standing wriggling slightly.

"Through the door, right and it's the third door on the left," Mary interjected.

"Thank you, my dear, er ..." reading off her nameplate, "... Mary, would you please be an angel and do me a small gin and it by the time I get back?"

"Certainly, ma'am."

"How'd it go in there, *ma'am*?" I asked, emphasising the 'ma'am'.

"Very well, Harry, thank you for asking. Now, must dash!"

"She's nice," Mary volunteered as she placed Gina's drink on the bar, "Better than that other arsehole, anyway, pardon my French."

"Yes, he's definitelay an arsehole. Oy've only known Mrs Gina for three days and she's definitelay one of the good 'uns."

"You er taking her to a hotel or all the way home ... cos I get off in a hour," Mary said coyly, "if you want to get a drink or maybe a bite to eat. Everything stays open really late around here."

"Oy'm married, Mary" holding up my wedding ring finger. "Anyway, how old are yow?"

"Twenty," she replied stiffly.

"Well, Oy've got children older than yow. Don't waste yowr time on old men, Mary, those that take up yowr offer, well, they only take, they don't give. Surely a pretty girl like yow must have a boyfriend of yowr own age back at home?"

"No, I haven't, not really. I used to have one but then I ... mucked it all up." She started to tear up and suddenly ran out from behind the bar and left the room running and crying at the same time.

"Bugger!" I said out loud and got off my stool to follow her. As I reached the door, Gina came in.

"Where did Mary go? She flew past me in tears. What did you say to her?"

"Well, she tried to chat me up. I showed her my ring and told her I was married and that I had kids older than her, and that she shouldn't go for older men, that she must know someone nearer her own age. She's only twenty. Anyway, she said she did have a boyfriend but she mucked it up. I was going to try and find her."

"I've got this, Harry, I think she was heading for the loo. You watch the fort."

I sat back on the barstool. The door opened from the boardroom and someone asked where Gina was.

"She's gone to the Ladies, loike, Oy'll tell her yow wanted her as soon as she gets back, roight?"

"Thank you."

A couple of minutes later Gina came through the door alone. "Mary's phoning her mum from one of the offices."

"They want you back in the boardroom. Rupert's still in there."

"Wish me luck."

"I wish you luck."

A couple of minutes later, the board emerged en mass from the boardroom in cheerful chatting groups. Mary still wasn't back from phoning her mum, nor had she told the waitresses to return, so I got behind the bar and served drinks at the bar for a while.

Gina stood with her father and a small group of supporters.

Mary came in through the door and headed straight for Gina and gave her an excited hug.

"I phoned Mum," she said breathlessly, loud enough for me to hear across the room, "and my Darren, well, he was my Darren until I dumped him. Well, he's not got a mum, see, and we've been friends ever since we went to school and he regards my mum like his mum. And you'll never guess but when I rung my Mum, Daz was actually there in the same room and Mum put him on and although he went out with that slut Heather Goddard once, he hadn't dated anyone else since because he still loved me. Isn't that wonderful?"

"It is, Mary, it's wonderful news."

"So I'm going home tomorrow, I should never have run away."

"Go and tell Harry the news, he thought he had upset you."

Mary ran to me, but I was was already

walking towards them, and she jumped into my arms. I just spun her around in a hug while she breathlessly repeated the same story she had told Gina.

Gina turned to the other board members, who were looking for an explanation.

"Oh, Mary's the niece, or cousin once removed or something, of Harry my driver. She ran away from home and her family were worried sick about her. It looks like she's going home. Pure coincidence meeting her like this but it's looking like a fairytale ending."

"Remarkable new driver you have, my dear," Fred said with a broad grin.

"Mmm, yes, Dad, he seems to have an affinity with finding solutions to people's problems, he definitely has hidden depths."

Gina smiled as we all watched Mary get her act together, smooth her dress down and get behind the bar. Just then the two young waitresses reappeared from where they had been resting and started working, asking the board members if they wanted drinks. It appeared most did.

Gina finished her drink and walked over to the bar, exchanging smiles with Mary who was preparing a couple of drinks and handing them to a waitress.

"Do you want a refill, ma'am?" Mary asked.

"No thanks, Mary. Please call me Gina, we've

hugged already, so no need to be so formal, these are the modern Seventies after all. So, we'll be off soon, once I say goodbye to my father. You going home to Mum tomorrow?"

"Yeah, this is only an agency job, not a real career. I work when they want me and they send me to night clubs or pubs to fill in for holidays or sick. No, I'm going home first thing in the morning. I can't wait to see Daz again."

"Where do you live?"

"I'm in digs just around the corner from here but my mum lives in Hertfordshire, er, Rickmansworth?"

"We are going to Buckinghamshire, Gina," I said quietly in Gina's ear, "And Rickmansworth could very easily be on our way."

"Mary, we're leaving in five minutes," Gina said, "how would you like to be driven from here to your digs in a beautiful Rolls-Royce, given help by me to pack up all your belongings and be driven home to your mother's home tonight, maybe while Daz is still waiting there for you?"

Mary's eyes lit up, looking from Gina to me and back again. "Really? You would do that?"

"Consider it Harry's 'bob-a-job' good deed of the day," Gina smiled.

"Mmm, no problem," I said, "but you're both sitting in the back on the way."

"Why, Harry?"

"Because, young lady, Oy'm drivin' oop front an' yow two girls'll be in the back gigglin' about the men in your loives and how yow enslave them and drive 'em crazy. And all the whoile Oy'm drivin' Oy'll be wishing Oy had a courtesy window that Oy could shuut out stuff that a self-respectin' bloke like me shouldn't hear."

"Right, I'm phoning Mum quickly and get her to keep Darren there, and then I'm ready to go. Julie! Here! I'm finishing early, you'll have to prepare the rest of the drinks and clean up after, all right?"

℞

We left Mary with her Mum and a touching reacquaintance with her boyfriend and they insisted we stay on for a cup of tea.

Somewhere in Hertfordshire, a mile or two north of Rickmansworth, from the passenger seat beside me, Gina asked me to pull into an unlit lay-by just ahead and switch off the engine for a minute.

"It's all right Gina, I know the way home from here, we'll be there in about half an hour."

"I know, but there's something I want you to do, need to do, before we go much further."

I pulled into the lay-by and switched off the engine.

"I want you to kiss me, Harry. Not a buzz or a peck on the lips but a full Frenchie, the type of kiss between lovers, long, hard and passionate enough to curl my toes and blow your own shoes and socks clean off! Please Harry. No promises, no recriminations, I just need you to kiss my face off and I'm asking you to do it now while I still have the nerve to go through with it."

I removed my driving gloves, leaned in and put my left hand behind her head and pulled her to me. Just before our lips touched, her face was lit up by a passing car, and I thought she looked beautiful, but also apprehensive, so I thought I would go gently and carefully and work slowly up to a Frenchie.

Our soft lips touched. I gently cradled the cheek of her face with my right hand, she placed her hands on my chest and grabbed the lapels of my jacket to pull me in as close as we could get to each other in the bucket seats of the Roller. Our lips parted during our kiss and hot tongues met and explored and savoured our respective tastes.

Gina's smaller hands then moved up to caress the back of my head and neck, while my thumb stroked her cheek. Our breathing rate increased, air noise audible through our noses as our kiss deepened and we extended our kiss for a long five minutes (or was it ten?) before we broke it off, both of us gasping for air and our hearts racing like Formula 1 podium winners.

She giggled as she caught her breath, a lovely sound to my ears.

"Thank you, Harry, I needed that, after seeing all that young true love filling the air at Mary's Mum's house."

"Yes, she's a nice kid and they look like they'll make a nice couple. I didn't say anything to Mary, but one of my customers in Watford was still looking for a Receptionist last Friday. I'll ring him tomorrow between appointments to see if it is still vacant."

"And I suppose you've got Mary's Mum's telephone number?"

"Got it just before we left."

"Well done, Harry, when it comes to fixing people's lives, you've got to be number one."

"I'm just the driver, Gina, you were the one who calmed Mary down, got her to call her Mum and suggested we get her home safely into Daz's arms."

"It only goes to show that we're a great team together."

"I guess we are." I agreed as I kissed her briefly before straightening up in our respective seats.

All the way home I could still feel the sensation of her lips on mine and the effect her kissing had on me. I couldn't help thinking that I was getting in deep and how I was going come away from this temporary escort arrangement without serious heartache all the way down the line?

℞

All Gina's stuff was already moved into my room, our room, presumably by Linda and Tom, we found as soon as we got back. I didn't dare ask if Fred and Pam knew.

Fred and his driver, the Young Tom, had long ago beaten us back from the board meeting, as his Jag was already parked and its bonnet stone cold in the garage by the time we got home.

Before we fell sleep on Wednesday night we agreed to talk about my company's prices for King & Son's orders during our hospital visit with Eric on Thursday night. Because we had already kissed long and hard earlier, she only wanted a quick cuddle and a soft kiss goodnight once we were ready to go to bed and sleep.

It didn't seem at all odd that were were sleeping platonically together, apparently with her household's approval. We were comfortable with each other even though we had only known met for the first time a couple of days before.

We were settling into a relationship like an old married couple, knowing that lines we had painlessly crossed, had further lines already drawn off that would need more negotiation to cross, if ever they were to be crossed during our temporary arrangement.

Chapter 6
Thursday 18 September 1975, 9.05am

INSTEAD OF GOING through the prices with Gina as originally planned, we had agreed to delay that until the evening.

So I drove off to see Stan Edmunds at Rawlings in Gloucester on Thursday morning, but only after checking with my guys back at the works that all deliveries could be made on Friday first thing.

I was also informed by Bob Andrews that the production guys had worked all night on the stainless to complete that part of the order and were continuing production to build up some stock ready to resupply on demand. The Sales Manager said that they could sell this as a new addition to our lines and could see several likely applications with existing customers. Bob had been keeping the Despatch Manager abreast of progress and everything would be loaded up tonight and on the road early in the morning to be timed to arrive at Rawlings by 6am on Friday.

Stan was delighted that we could deliver

everything as promised early the next morning. So we sat in his office, and we went through all the figures in the quotation and reached final agreement on the deal with a handshake, confirming that the next order through would be in a week's time and would be for about three months' supply to maintain a healthy stock balance, followed by a month's worth every month.

"Great that we got this sorted out today, Harry. I'm sure that this is the quickest and sweetest supply deal we've ever negotiated at Rawlings, so I really appreciate what you've done. Steer yourself well clear of here tomorrow and Monday, though," Stan told me, "all our bad suppliers are picking up their overpriced stock and all the new suppliers are bringing in the new. So far your company are the only ones that have fully filled the orders and production are happy to have weekly deliveries in future and have the flexibility to make adjustments. Now, we need a new receptionist, Harry, we usually only keep them there for a couple of years or so and move them higher up the food chain, so don't take this as a challenge, but everything else you've done for us is first class." said Stan.

"Hold that thought, Stan, I did have someone special that I had earmarked for a company in Watford, but I haven't said anything to anyone yet. I think she might be willing to look further afield. She's only 20, she's very well turned out and she's worked in London as a cocktail barkeep and managing a team of cocktail waitresses at Tremblett's group HQ. She's bright, flexible, wants to enlarge her horizons, but has a feckless boyfriend that needs some serious 'umph' behind him to get him going and then keep him running. Apparently the kid she loves enjoys tinkering about with engines and bikes but hasn't the school certificates necessary to secure an engineering apprenticeship."

Stan just shook his head that I was able to come up with something so quick, "And they'd move here just like that?"

"Well, I know just the two landladies nearby your factory here who could accommodate them, separately, five nights a week. This girl's cute, very attractive and committed romantically, but I think that she'd do well working her way up your food chain here as I'm certain she's smart as a button and already experienced authority in handling staff and dealing with difficult board members."

"Ha! You think I'm difficult? You should see the others!" Stan laughed, slappin me on the back. "Well, we are expanding our production lines, Harry, and we've shift overseers here who won't take any crap from anyone we behind their ears. That might well suit your girl's boyfriend if he needs a firm hand. Great opportunities here for progression beyond the assembly lines, too. Set your girl up to visit us and I'll tee up our Personnel Department to interview them this afternoon if you can get her or both of them here."

"I'll do it now." I picked up a desk phone and dialled nine in front of the number I had written on the back of a card in my pocket.

"Mary? ... Oh hello Mandy, it's Harry, from last night? ... Yes, you're right, Gina's a pretty special lady for a toff, in fact she's a pure sweetheart. Look, can you get Mary to the phone if she's there? Thanks ... oh hi, Mary, how would you like to work in the beautiful country town of Gloucester? ... in Reception to start with for maybe a couple of years, then there's training available to work your way up in the back office? ... yes? And they've got plenty of work for Darren too, factory assembly work to start with, but this is a first class engineering company, so modern working conditions, good labour relations ... yes, very progressive, this company is always at the leading edge, so his progress is really up to him and how much he wants to work. ... This afternoon, yes. I can come pick you both up and get you here and back home again safe and sound. No, it's no trouble, completely at your disposal, in fact, if you like it here and they like you, you could start almost straight away.... They won't just like you, Mary, they'll love you, I guarantee it, and you'll love it here too. See you in two hours, then. Bye."

Harry turned to Stan. "They can be here this afternoon by 2pm, both ready to start on Monday morning if you like the look of them."

"And the digs you mentioned?" laughed Stan, shaking his head.

"While your people are interviewing them, I'll sort out their separate digs. They'll both be safe there and I assure you, with these two ladies they will never oversleep, they'll get a good night's sleep Sunday night to Friday mornings and they will be absolutely mothered to death in between!"

"Go on, Harry, go fetch them and I'll chalk this one up to experience. But one of these days I'll be finding some way of coming up with a challenge that you can't meet!"

Mary and Darren were both offered and accepted jobs that afternoon and had been introduced to their sweet landladies and were ready to start their new careers the next week. I took them home that afternoon and happily fixed up with to drive them and their suitcases to Gloucester early on Sunday night.

Our delivery lorry was set to leave at 4am the

next day, Friday, and the Rawlings warehouse and stores manager had Bob Arnold's number in case of any problems and our Despatch in Birmingham even had a spare van and driver on standby in case Rawlings had left anything off their original order. The account was that valuable to us and Rawlings had a great reputation that we were all interested in maintaining and promoting.

Thursday night at the hospital, while visiting the comatose Eric, Gina and I went through my company's proposals for supplying fixings to King's that had arrived over the fax on Wednesday evening after we had left the office. I pointed out the savings in cash flow and flexibility of supply by having monthly deliveries and 30-day invoices rather than quarterly supplies and invoices up front. The Company had gone over to digital sizes some 10 years earlier but still had unused stores of AF and Whitworth sizes, which I offered to buy up at scrap value and collect when we made our first delivery. I was sure Bert knew exactly how much old stock he had.

I did take those redundant screws off her hands, offering the fair price of £30 for the lot of them, which Bert the storeman had earlier urged she accepted as he was certain that they will never find a use for them. I told her that we would be donating them to a charity that sends such material over to the Commonwealth countries in Africa and Asia who still find them useful in their emerging economies. She offered to donate them in that case, saying that Bert would appreciate the extra room.

Friday night we met the King & Son office crew at the pub for a social drink. We decided that we might as well go there as if we were a couple, arm in arm. That caused quite a few interested looks and a buzz of whispers.

When Gina went to the loo while I ordered our drinks at the bar, Polly pulled me to one side.

"Well, does she?"

"Does she what?" I asked as I smiled in all innocence.

"You know ... bite!"

"I never tell tales, Polly," and I smiled at her with a twinkle in my eye.

"I knew it! Where?"

"Out of sight ... twice."

"Ooh, lovely. I'm very happy for you, and to think that I was the one who sort of got you two lovebirds together, I feel all shivery all over," she said, "with romance in the air."

"Well, we'll keep it to ourselves, shall we?"

"Our little secret?"

"Ours."

Polly ran back to her friends, giggling, I imagined our little secret would be all over the pub within ten minutes, no, make that thirty seconds.

"What was that all about?" Gina asked, seeing Polly running off, leaning in close to me as the pub was so noisy, so close that I could tell she had reapplied her subtle but heady perfume.

She had a hand on my shoulder, so I moved one of my hands halfway up her back to hold her close.

With my lips close to her ear I whispered, "When Polly told me on Monday that you were a woman responsible for buying supplies, I imagined an old fire-breathing dragon from accounts, so I innocently asked if you bite, and she said, 'oh yes, she bites all right'. And just now she asked if you really did bite, and I told her a gentleman never tells ... but I must've smiled a little at the memory."

"And you gave me away, you rat!" she laughed and shoulder bumped me.

"Sort of, er, well, Polly asked exactly where, so I just said, 'out of sight', which made her giggle and then, because I am so proud of you, how you moved us on as friends so quickly, that I added ..."

"'Twice!' I thought that's what I heard at the end. I'll never be able..."

"Yes you will, Gina, because your stock just went up ten-fold. You're not just the boss's daughter and a hard arse boss when you need to be, you've reminded people that you're naturally human and hot stuff too, and if anyone wants to take you on, they better be fireproof."

"And are you 'asbestos' Harry, immune to naked flames?"

"No, baby, I'm just just hovering here getting as close to the flames as I can get, enjoying the burn. I may look cool on the outside but I'm a raging furnace of emotions inside!"

"Let's get out of here, H? We've done enough PR bit for one night."

"Sure, let's go."

We drank up, said our goodbyes and left the pub holding hands, knowing that the subject of the conversations behind us would be about the Boss Lady and the Salesman, who had breezed into their lives only four and a half short days earlier and left as Lovers.

That night we kissed as we cuddled in bed. Boy, did we kiss, it took all of my resolve to keep our romancing to just kissing and cuddling safe zones.

On Saturday we listened on the radio to the Liverpool game together, an expected 3-0 defeat for the Villa, who were finding the first division hard going. The rest of the day we got ready for the local Conservative Party evening fundraising event.

I have never been particularly political, but I generally always voted Labour as they were the party that did most good in the area where I lived and was brought up. It was interesting, meeting lots of people, but I found it bewildering too, as for most of the evening I was surrounded by the businessmen's wives who, because I had said I was only 'escorting' Gina to functions while her husband was indisposed, the women were fascinated to find out if I did this escorting professionally or not.

I just told them that I knew her father Fred from various trade associations, was a regular supplier to the King & Son's company, was conveniently unmarried and at a loose end whilst travelling. Therefore I was only escorting her on a purely platonic basis while her husband was incapacitated, but as she was a beautiful lady through and through I was enjoying her company all the same.

I got the impression that once my time was over with Gina, I would get offers to escort some of these wives, if that was something I wanted to get involved in.

I wasn't sure what I might be getting into, so I kept my responses light and humorous, hopefully, and only lightly flirting with the women and avoiding being alone with any of them. They all seemed dangerous to me!

To say Gina had giggling fits most of the evening, amused at my clear discomfort, was an understatement.

I paid her back in bed by finding out she was extremely ticklish, the first time I had ventured outside so-called safe zones, and we snogged long and hard until sleep claimed us.

Chapter 7
Sunday 21 September 1975, 1.35pm

ON SUNDAY AFTERNOON we prepared for a garden party at the Kings' family home, something they put on a couple of times a year during the summer for the factory staff.

That Sunday was a glorious day, both weather wise and also the clear enjoyment that the day seemed to bring to all the participants. Once it got under way, Gina and I hardly saw each other, such were the demands put upon us, particularly Gina.

I sat out of the way for a while, and was joined by a woman of about my own age, who owned up to being the accounting bookkeeper at King & Son, and she put me through a bit of a grilling, but eventually agreed with me that my figures and approach to the supplies that I offered were sound and an improvement on what they had before, but she made it clear that she was keeping a close watch on me.

Being at a loose end, I decided to add to the entertainment by driving the kids and their mums the short distance around the gravel drive for half an hour in the Rolls-Royce, then young Tom took over the driving for me and he said he would hand over to his granddad after a while, who was himself keen to get behind the wheel of the Roller, so I soon found that I was a free agent again for the rest of the afternoon!

I tried to find Gina during this unexpected period of freedom but was waylaid by Fred, who wanted me to accompany him around the formal garden and talk about Gina's depression of late and how he felt I had begun the process of lifting her out of it. He thanked me for loaning my Roller to the two Toms and entertaining the guests.

I guess I waited for the guillotine to drop that they'd finally had more than enough of me, but Fred just encouraged me.

"Keep up the good work, Harry, you're doing great. Gina's like a new young woman again, and we love her like that. Never seen her so happy in years. Oh, and I've got a couple of other companies that want you to call on them next week. There's a pigeonhole for mail and messages that we all use just outside the kitchen, one of the slots has now got your name on, and I've slipped the details of these companies in there for you. Check it on the way out of the house and when you back in again as that's where we'll leave any messages or mail. We all use the kitchen door rather than the front door!"

I disappeared late afternoon to ferry the excited kids Mary and Darren from Rickmansworth up to Gloucester and didn't get back until 9pm.

By that time on Sunday night Gina was exhausted, from all the organising and hand shaking she'd done all day.

We went to bed early and we just spooned. I pulled her in tight and buried my nose in her fragrant hair, then kissed her neck. She sighed and pulled my hand to her breast and held it there. I kneaded her breasts in wonder at how they could be both firm and soft, the first breasts I had been allowed to touch since my marriage ended. She twisted herself enough to kiss me over her shoulder, a short French kiss with me still massaging one of her breasts, my hand held in place by both her hands.

"Goodnight, H. You're becoming my shining knight."

She kissed me again and snuggled her back into my front before dropping off to sleep almost immediately, the poor woman had given everything for her company today.

I don't think she heard me whisper, "And you're becoming my night and day."

It took me a lot longer to drop off, my hand relaxed from holding her breast but, as I tried to remove them, Gina snuffled in her sleep and held my hands close to her hot breast. It took me a lot longer to drop off to sleep after that!

Monday was a quiet night in for both of us after work, sitting and relaxing in pleasant company with Fred and Pam in their sitting room until we declared an early bedtime.

Gina came to bed wearing just a pair of knickers and I licked and sucked those magnificent breasts for fully two hours before we slept in each other's arms.

I knew I could never tire of holding her, kissing her, being with her. Without being able to tell her in so many words, I was clear in my physical demonstrations that I was fast falling in love with Mrs Eric Tremblett, a woman I had known for just over a week. I knew it would take me a lifetime to get over her, while Mavis was now just a distant, slightly irritating, memory.

Tuesday night we both drove up to the Wolves' ground at Molineux to watch a lively local derby which ended in a 0-0 draw, where I felt the Villa were lucky to hang onto that precious point. We had access to the Wolves' board room before and after the game. We spoke to some old players who were surprisingly chatty and full of interesting and amusing stories concerning derby matches and were able to chat to both team managers and a few current players after the game. Gina was simply beautiful, holding onto my arm, and took full part in the conversations and managed to look not the least bit bored. She was clearly the moth that attracted the attention to us, and I certainly had a marvellous time.

We visited her husband a couple of evenings during the week and it seemed that it no longer caused her to be upset and we mostly sat around the bed and chatted about our separate workday activities. The consultant neurosurgeon did stay behind his normal working hours on Thursday night to speak to us at the very start of visiting hours.

Gina insisted I remain present, even though not related to the patient, but all the consultant wanted to say was to confirm after numerous tests that there was no change in Tremblett's condition, any possibility of recovery was still hopeless but the legal wheels were turning slowly so nothing was likely to happen for several more weeks, if not months.

Saturday we went to my home stamping ground of Villa to play "Brummagem" City, where we won 2-1 in front of nearly 54,000 ecstatic fans.

It was certainly a first experience for me to enjoy some special time in one of our own executive boxes and meet the board of directors of the football club I loved after the game. I guessed they didn't get that many guests who were quite as dyed in the claret and blue as I was, nor a guest accompanied by such a beautiful woman as Gina.

The way Gina looked at me I knew she appreciated how I felt about the experience and I held her in my arms afterwards, just before we drove back, saying I really couldn't thank her enough. Gina said that being with me for that afternoon was an enjoyable experience for her too, recognising how much I enjoyed myself.

A couple of weeks later we drove the Rolls-Royce down to see her son, young teenager Giles Tremblett. I found him a sensitive boy who didn't want to be cuddled by his mother in front of his peers and, I noticed, he kept Gina between me and him and was noticeably nervous of me. In the tea room, Gina had to leave us to go powder her nose.

"Hi, sport," I said to Giles, "Now your mother's not with us I want you to know that I am not trying to be your father and will never be. I simply don't know how long I'll be with your mother as friends. We are not really romantically linked, I am not really her boyfriend, just someone helping her through this no-man's-land between broken marriage and widowhood. I am escorting her to various functions and acting as if there is some romance between us to protect her from the wolves out there who might find her vulnerable without your father to protect her."

Giles looked at me with his big eyes and said nothing, just nodded in understanding at each point.

"Now, having said all that, I do happen to like your Mum, I really like her a lot and we are developing into good friends. I hope that, whatever happens after this escorting business isn't necessary for her any more, that we will remain good friends forever. I was a kid once and I have a son in his early twenties who was a boy your age when I last lived at home as a family. I do recognise that as male bodies change from boy to man, at the beginning of your teens as you are now, it can be a very worrying and emotional time for you, especially as you soon won't have a father to share things with that you are reluctant to raise with your mother. I know you may find things you can't talk to your mum about, like the urges you may feel, your developing sexuality and issues about masturbation, whether you should or shouldn't."

Giles' eyes got bigger and he swallowed a lot.

"You don't know me, Giles and you don't trust me, and why should you? I could be a predator, of either your mum or even you … there's all kinds of horrible dangers out there,

Giles. When I was a kid my dad called them the bogeyman. I am not one of those, I'm as straight forward a chap as you can get, but you don't have to take my word for it, just be careful, take care of yourself first and foremost. So, if you ever want to discuss things with me that you can't approach your mother about comfortably, then I will meet you somewhere public and safe, in full view, yet where we can also talk openly and privately. Bring some friends along for safety in numbers if you like and I can drive you all to a milk bar or tea shop where we can find a quiet corner in a public place and talk about your concerns, all right?"

Giles nodded again. Then he stretched out both hands and I stretched out mine in response. He shook one of my hands with both hands quite seriously as if he was all grown up and said,

"You're all right, Mr H. I know my Mum likes you, she's mentioned in her letters that she's comfortable with you and she has left me with you just now, so she clearly trusts you with her only son. Yes, you are right, I do have issues, I'm a kid, and I do have things happing to me that my mum would be the last person I'd like to speak to about. Maybe I will take you up on your offer and we can have a chat once in a while. I know some of my friends would get a kick out of being driven to a tuck shop in a Roller." He smiled and I laughed with him.

I told Giles that because I could often go a fortnight between visits to my office, I do phone into work all the time and take messages, so I gave him one of my cards. Otherwise, I told him, I already let Polly at King's have my weekly schedule, so he could ring there if he ever needed to get in contact with me. Also that I was happy that he let his mother know that he was taking me into his confidence, when and where we were meeting and whether the general gist of any conversations we had were to remain confidential or not.

And very soon after that conversation, we did chat from time to time and I gave him down to earth explanations of why he actually seemed to be coping well with what personal problems he was facing, growing up in the stressful environment of a boarding school while effectively having only one parent.

I found Giles was even more fragile than his mother had been when we first met. I felt that in a short passage of time, we also became good friends, although I found out much later that he wasn't always as forthcoming with me as I was with him, especially as there were times I felt we could discuss my feelings towards his mother.

Gina and I carried on seeing each other in this cat and mouse game we were playing of escort/boyfriend for months, breaking the routine of being at the centre of attention with weekends away from home, some of which I was happy to initiate and pay for. Sometimes we included Giles in our outings, but he was a kid who mostly preferred his own company.

We went on sailing weekends, pony trekking, painting nude still life male models in watercolours at a university art class (one of her favourite memories after getting over the initial shock of it), fell walking, camping, cooking and visiting one of the new Sussex wineries, seeing the harvesting and fermenting process and sampling the wines made in previous years.

Gina had mentioned she enjoyed singing, so I discovered the existence of and joined the local town's choral society; I got roped into droning on in the bass section at the back out of the way, while Gina sang solos at the front, and every quarter we togged up in evening wear and helped put on concerts for local audiences. We were enjoying life and we thoroughly enjoyed each other's company.

We slept together, where we petted and cuddled but we drew the line at penetrative sex. As far as I was concerned she was still a married woman and in the era in which I was brought up it was a threshold of cheating that I simply wouldn't cross, even if her husband was a vegetable in hospital with his immediate future existence something that his relatives squabbled over. I felt we had developed clear and undisguised feelings for each other and l know I looked forward to seeing her at the end of each day. Together we seemed to be touching each other all the time and holding hands wherever we went. And the days when we were together enjoying each other's company seemed wonderfully endless.

Chapter 8
Tuesday 6 January 1976, 7.15pm

W E VISITED HER hubby Eric at least once a week and usually twice where our busy schedules allowed, for almost four months until the courts finally ruled on Thursday 6 January that life support could be switched off on Wednesday 14 January 1976 at 5pm.

The Judge ruled that there was no appeal to his decision but would allow just over a week of life support to allow all parties to brace themselves for the inevitable.

Then, the very next day, on Wednesday morning, a week before the expected shut down, a communication was circulated by the Company Secretary of an Extraordinary Board Meeting of the Trembletts Group to discuss rumours of a hostile takeover bid.

Villa had earned a third round FA Cup Replay that evening against second Division side Southampton at Villa Park and we had originally both planned on going.

My new friend at the club, Pat Matthews, had reserved tickets for Gina and I on Monday when they went on sale. My season ticket only guaranteed me a seat for league games.

"I have to go to the board meeting, Harry," Gina said apologetically when I rang her back after she left a message with my 11 o'clock appointment.

"Daddy's away, so I have to be there. Hostile bids mean aggressive, timely and expensive repostes. I expect there's plenty of my supporting board members coming, even at such short notice, so I'll be perfectly safe. You can still go to your match."

I knew where my loyalties lay. Fred and Pam were on holiday in the Caribbean until the end of next week. She couldn't use either of the Toms to drive her because while Fred and Pam were away and the duties in the garden were minimal in January, so the domestic help were also departed for warmer climes, leaving Gina and I to happily fend for ourselves for the two weeks.

I didn't need to go to every single match my team were involved in, while I did want to protect Gina from any hostile environment. That hostility wasn't just physical in form, I had no real fears on that point, but emotionally I wanted to boost her confidence before the meeting and then calm her down after a couple of hours of open hostility and scorning disrespect from a bunch of dinosaurs who knew their days were numbered once Gina could finally exercise Eric's stockholding into shaking up and modernising the board, which would include sacking all of Eric's old Trembletts and Collins cronies.

"No, honey, I wouldn't enjoy a single minute of the match knowing thatbyou had to face the Tremblett board on your own and I could've, should've been with you," I said. "We've been to three monthly meetings so far, including your initial meeting, and you can cut the 'females belong in the kitchen and the bedroom not the boardroom', attitude towards you with a knife. I could cope with allowing you to go without me if your father was there, but as we know he can't be, so I'm driving you there and providing a shoulder for you on the way back."

"Honey, you're a treasure."

"Just hold that thought all day and, when you are in that meeting, just remember there's someone the other side of that door who believes in you and cares about you."

I hadn't taken into account the late shopping nights for the January sales still in full swing in the West End, so we arrived a little late because of the traffic, then I found I couldn't park nearby because of "Police No Parking" cones all around Tremblett House. After circling the block in a fruitless search for a space, which made her two more minutes late, I dropped Gina off at the front entrance, then drove around to find somewhere further afield to park.

It was a mild evening, but the weather was forecast as changeable and I had to bear in mind that on the previous day London had 6mm rain fall overnight, while the week before the worst gales to hit the British Isles for over twenty years had caused 21 deaths just a hundred miles north east of London. So I took with me the James Smith & Son brolly I normally kept locked in the boot, just in case it was raining when we left to return to the car. I had to drive around for twenty minutes and eventually parked about five or six minutes' brisk walk away from the office building.

Julie, the lone bar server in the board member's lounge, was agitated when I reached the board room area.

"Thank god you're here Harry," she gushed, her voice full of panic and her pretty young face contorted in anguish, "I was frantic and didn't know what to do other than wait for you. I think they put a Micky in Mrs Tremblett's drink, because within a couple of minutes she was out of it and they virtually dragged her into the board room and locked the door behind them," she recounted breathlessly. "I tried to ring the police but the phone ain't working either in here or in any on the offices off the corridor. I waited 'cos I thought you'd know what to do. I have a key to the board room."

She walked to the door while I gripped my brolly and, as an afterthought, picked up a heavy half-full bottle of Champagne by the neck from an ice bucket on a table I passed.

"How many?" I asked with a growl.

"Four of them, Harry, the nasty Collins' twins, Mr Bambridge and the secretary Mr Cooper. I was expecting the whole board, but only these four at first and then Mrs Tremblett turned up.

"Unlock and stand back, Julie," I growled and then I kicked the door open.

In front of me, Gina was spreadeagled naked on the board room table, apparently completely senseless, her clothes discarded on the floor. The bare-legged Collins' twins were holding up Gina's legs and Cooper, the Company Secretary, was raping her at the edge of the table. Behind him was Bambridge, also without his trousers on. He was the first to half turn to face me and didn't even see the champagne bottle hit him across the face with his nose taking the brunt of it.

I could see what was happening in slow motion as it appeared his nose just disappeared into his face, his cheekbone shattered and his jawbone broken in more than one place, displaced teeth flying up and down like in a sport's action replay. At the same time, champagne foamed around my wrist through the open neck and shot up my arm. Bambridge collapsed to the ground, so I could concentrate my focus on Cooper, who was now half-turned facing me with a look of horror on his face. My peripheral vision could see his disgusting wet dick waving around that he had been violating my Gina with.

I was surprised the bottle hadn't shattered from the first blow, clearly it was stronger than fragile bone and cartilage, but I had carried through with my stroke and it would take time to draw the bottle up, cocked ready to reuse as an offensive weapon again.

Instead, I put all my effort into my left arm now behind me, at the end of which was my Smith & Son umbrella, which I gripped about the middle of the shaft. It was a sturdy steel tube and framed umbrella with a solid crome-plated tip with a rounded point. I thrust it at his face at an upward angle. He had no time to raise his hands to defend himself, so the umbrella connected first with his lower front teeth, which exploded from either side of his jaw, then punctured his tongue, entered his soft pallet and interfered with his spinal nerve column at the back of his head. He shivered, as if on the end of an electric shock, and collapsed like a deflated gay sex doll, if such a monstrocity exists.

Thrusting away with my left side, while propelling myself forward, I effectively swung the champagne bottle from low and behind me, swinging it at the Collins twin on my right. He did manage to release Gina's left leg, and lift his right hand up to fend off the blow, but my rage, the arc of travel, the leverage at the very end of my outstretched arm, along with putting much of my body weight behind it, made his gesture futile and just gave the surgeons a challenge to remove his broken hand from the ruination of his fractured skull and jumble of bone peppered scrambled tissue.

And still that damned bottle didn't break. This time the last of the contents foamed up my arm or gushed to the now slippery floor underfoot.

The other twin had dropped Gina's leg and tried to make a run for it, and might have made it if he had previously fully removed his trousers rather than just drop them, but they were still snugly enveloped around his ankles and all I had to do was fall backward onto the cushion of the fallen Bambridge and bang the handle of the umbrella on the floor, allowing the other Collins twin to fall on the umbrella tip, which stabbed into his flabby torso around his sternum. It didn't go all the way through the body, as the tubular frame gave way from the impact, the penetrating shaft avoided his lungs but otherwise the complex structure of splintered umbrella frame exploded in all directions and made a complete mess of his innards which were encountered along the way.

I got up still holding the now empty bottle and surveyed the scene. The left hand Collins was rolling in agony, the umbrella embedded deep in his fat guts. I had been sitting on Bambridge and he was completely out for the count, his face and the front of his white dress shirt a mass of blood and splintered bone. The right hand Collins was lying in a pool of blood around his unmoving head. Cooper was sitting up with his head against the table, his hands held up against his ruined face, moaning in pain. I hoisted the bottle one final time and brought it down with a smash on the top of his head, his skull caved in like a soft boiled egg; he shut up immediately like a squawking radio with the plug pulled suddenly from the mains.

Gina was completely out of it, her body limp and relaxed. Her eyes were shut but she was still breathing, but I was worried that her breathing was so shallow. I held her to me, supporting her flopping head, her body so relaxed she could have been dead.

I turned to Julie, who stood open mouthed at the doorway of the board room.

"Find a public phone box, Julie, call 999, tell them we need police and at least two ambulances. There are five casualties, one a female drug and rape victim who is unconscious, and four males, all serious injuries possible fatalities, or they will be by the time they bloody well get here."

"Harry, I can't say I'd blame you," Julie said more calmly thazn I felt, "but you've done enough damage in a matter of moments that can be explained away with the scene you saw and a good witness to back you up, but don't do anything while I've gone that will take you away from Mrs Tremblett at a time when she will need you more than anyone with eyes can see she that already does."

"It's all right, Julie, the red mist's gone, I just need professional help for Gina now and I will spend my time getting her decent and respectable again while you're gone."

"OK Harry, I'm here for both of you, all right? These scum won't be free for many many years to come, we'll see to that."

I could barely see through my eyes for the tears, but I found Gina's bra, dress and coat and put them on her while I propped her up on the table. Her knickers and stockings were torn up so there was no point in putting her garter back on. I put them on a chair for evidence of the attack on her and rape and left her shoes and garter belt on a chair near the door for convenience while I carried the unconscious Gina through to the lounge and sat her in a more comfortable chair while I awaited the return of Julie. The wait seemed interminable.

She came in with the first two ambulance men on scene. They could see the carnage and headed in there first.

"They made me wait outside the entrance to guide them through," Julie explained, "how's Gina?"

"She's still out of it, but she's breathing."

"Hopefully, she won't remember any of this ... and hopefully, you won't blame her for what happened, Harry."

"No, I won't blame Gina, this was partly my fault letting her come in here on her own. It was never her fault, Julie."

"Honey, if you were with her when she came in, you'd be as much out of it as she is now."

"Of course, you're right," I agreed, "just got to wait for the police. Look, Julie, if the police take me away will you —?"

"Of course," Julie said, gently squeezing my shoulder, "I'll make sure to accompany her to the hospital and call my boss and Mr King."

"No, Mr King is on a cruise in the West

Indies and cannot be reached. Here is my solicitor's card." I thumbed through my wallet until I found it. "He's also the family solicitor. Tell him what nick they're taking me to."

As it turned out, the Metropolitan Police were brilliant, very supportive and understanding from the moment they arrived, assessed the scene with no more than a glance and heard and believed Julie's explanation. They knew I wasn't going anywhere other than be with Gina and she was definitely going to hospital.

While the officer questioned me, as Gina was being examined by the ambulance men, Julie explained that this was clearly a conspiratorial attack on Mrs Tremblett set up by a limited number of board members on one vulnerable female.

"Look, if this was a normal board meeting, there would be paperwork, agendas, reports on the table. I thought it was strange that only I turned up, we normally have three waitresses, even when it is short notice like this one. Also, if it was a proper board meeting, there would be up to 16 members present, with a line of four or five limos parked outside. Here's a list of board members and their contact details," she pulled a sheet from a folder kept behind the bar. She looked at me, adding, "Some meetings certain members who do not have drivers, are incoherent and need cabs home, so we need their addresses." She turned to the policeman and added, "The drivers usually stay with their cars, but Mr Crabtree is regarded by the Chairman Mr King and his daughter here, Mrs Tremblett, as an equal, even like family."

The policeman regarded me with a raised eyebrow, "And your relationship with Mrs Tremblett, Sir?"

"I'm her boyfriend, not the hired help. She's someone I'd want to spend every available hour with, so I enjoy driving her around to meetings in my own Rolls-Royce."

He nodded, "I can catch up with you at the hospital?"

"I'll be there until she's released, Officer."

He looked at the ambulance men. One looked up.

"She's breathing, but we'll get her on oxygen when we take her down to the ambulance. I expect they'll pump her stomach to remove whatever agent they've given her, Sir, put her on a drip and keep her in for observation overnight."

"Can I follow you to the hospital, I presume St Thomas?"

"Yeah, St Thomas it is."

I gave the officer my business card. "I have written my home phone number and registration of my blue and silver Rolls-Royce on the back. I'd rather take the car to the hospital and not leave it here gathering parking tickets."

He acknowledged with a nod and let me follow the ambulance men and Gina on their stretcher.

I grasped Julie by the shoulders and kissed her cheek before following Gina, "Thank you for your help with Gina, Jools, you're a treasure."

"I didn't know what else to do," she said helplessly.

"You did good, honey, really good."

Chapter 9
Wednesday 14 January 1976, 7pm

Gina and I were ready prepared for an all night vigil, with just the two of us being present when Eric's life support was turned off, but Eric slipped away in just a matter of minutes, as if he wanted to go wherever he was heading. It was a relief to us and also to the hospital staff who had looked after him for so long and for so little reward for our efforts.

It had taken Gina about five days to recover from whatever Micky Finn had been given to her, with the hospital saying that chloral hydrate was the principle ingredient and a number of barbiturates, probably from several different brands of ground up sleeping tablets. Apparently mixing it with ethanol makes it work faster, drowsy within minutes, comatose in twenty to forty minutes.

Fortunately she was out completely when she was raped and had no recollection of what happened, not even any soreness, although she was weak as a kitten and more asleep than awake for the first couple of days and tired easily for

193

up to a week afterwards. I was concerned about pregnancy but Gina insisted that she was on the Pill and by the following Wednesday she heard the results of the tests that she was absolutely clear of any sexually transmitted diseases.

Somehow, I managed not to kill any of the four attackers but Bambridge had to have much painful reconstructive surgery on his face for months. Cooper was paralysed below the neck and would never walk again, his brain damage also meant that he had trouble talking and with his short-term memory. He was married with children, but was soon divorced and ostracised by his former family. William Collins was no longer an identical twin even after extensive surgery. His left hand was never the same so he would have had to give up playing golf even if he hadn't gone to gaol. His twin David Collins actually had least life threatening wounds and made almost made a complete a recovery although his digestion apparently was never quite the same again.

The two Collins were convicted of conspiring and being accessories to rape and each got six years, serving three. Cooper pleaded not guilty, that he was coerced into it by the others but, as his name was on every piece of paperwork connected with the offence, was convicted for 12 years, but being a paraplegic, that was a life sentence in itself. He was never actually released, dying in hospital with complications following a collapsed lung after only eighteen months.

Bambridge was considered the instigator and ringleader and got 15 years for his part in the aggravated rape.

All four were eventually prosecuted for fraud once Gina and her accountants got their hands on the company books.

Gina made a full recovery, with her only memories being of feeling woozy in the lounge and waking up about ten hours later in the hospital with me holding her hand.

When it came to Eric's funeral about a week later, I wanted to stay away, but Gina insisted that she needed my support, so I went with her. The funeral was well attended by Eric's relatives, and we went back with quite a crowd to Eric and their house for the wake, if only for the sandwiches. After everyone was gone, Fred and Pam, with Tom and Linda, chased us away from the clearing up and were encouraged to spend some time together.

As we drove home, well, to Fred and Pam's home, Gina took my hand.

"I want you to make love to me tonight, Harry. Now that Eric's truly gone, I feel a free woman at last to let myself go in every sense of the word, and the only man I want to let go with is you, Harry, you."

For a moment I wasn't sure what to say. At this time of night there was only ten minutes' driving time between the two houses and we had already spent the first five minutes in reflective silence. When I didn't immediately reply, she squeezed my hand and carried on talking.

"I know we've almost been living as 'man and wife' since, well, since within about 12 hours of us first meeting, but...." she giggled weakly, so I squeezed her hand back.

"Darling," I started, but she cut me off.

"I don't know if l believe in love at first sight, Harry, but I know I love you, that I trust you with my heart, my life, my son, my company and ... I hope ... our children, and our —"

"Gina, my darling," I interrupted her, "I fell in love with you the moment you walked down those steps at King's on that first day. I first fell in love with your ankles, your calves, your knees — and I didn't even see your knees until you sat in my car. Before we even shook hands I was captivated by your face, your eyes, the very way you hold yourself and simply hearing your voice gives me a tingle up my spine every time I hear you. So I do believe in love at first sight, and every single sight of you, every sentence I hear you speak, every breath that you take, every scent of you that I breathe, I am becoming even more captivated by you. I know I've loved you for four months, I love you now and I will always love you."

"Oh darling man, I'm so pleased!"

And Gina started to cry.

We were on the A40 and, although we were only minutes from home, I pulled into the next lay-by, switched the engine off and held her.

We kissed long and hard, then I was showered with many kisses and deep, passionate kisses again and again.

Soon we were laughing and crying but with tears of joy not sorrow. As soon as she started laughing through the tears, I released her and restarted the engine, checked the non-existent traffic for anything coming and pulled away towards our home.

"Home, 'James'," she said, "and don't spare the horsepower!"

We showered together for the first time but almost as soon as we soaped each other up we had to stop as Gina developed stomach cramps and realised her period had started.

"Oh damn! I'm not due until Monday. Oh Harry, I thought we would have three days of heavenly bliss before my period started."

She was in tears but I held her tightly and we dried each other off and we were soon in bed heavily kissing each other before she decided to give me a blow job. I pulled her back as she tried to burrow under the covers.

"Honey, I think this is a sign that we both need to wait for that special moment. We've been making love in some form or another for over four months. We are both certain of our love for each other and we are not under any time pressure here to consummate this relationship."

"I could still suck you off, H," she said looking me in the eye, even though I could tell she was suffering from cramps, her eyes wet with tears. I had slept with this wonderful woman through three periods and knew how painful they sometimes were for her, especially at the outset.

"You, my lovely, are going nowhere other than in my loving embrace," I told her firmly but lovingly as I held just as firmly. "If you cannot enjoy us going past second base for our first time, then why should I?"

"But I would enjoy it, honey, honestly I would, just as you would if the shoe was on the other foot."

"You're already cramping up, Gina. Just let us hold and touch and kiss and love as we have, and hold this over until we can clear our minds and go for it. I am more than ready for us to make love but I want to completely remove that first special moment from any association with Eric's death or his funeral. We can say this is his last day in our lives, that from the next dawn we are completely free from our former spouses and the rest of our lives are ours."

"You're right, honey. I'm not physically or mentally at my best right now, the stress of the funeral, the realisation that I have a new life to live must've have brought me on. I do love you, H, and I want a new start with you being in the forefront of my life."

"Pick a day, a night or a weekend in one or two weeks' time, Gina, and we can make it a special occasion for both us, something that both of us can remember as an event in itself. Our first time as lovers with no holds barred, the first in a long lifetime of every one of our nights being as good as the first."

So she decided that we would have a long weekend, Friday to Monday, in early February in Barcelona. She planned that we would do what we had always done on the weekend, except that Saturday night and Sunday morning we would make physical love to each other.

We flew out in the morning and we had a good relaxing time on the Friday and during the day on Saturday, telling each other by word and whisper, touch and gesture, that we were each in love with the other. Once we had committed ourselves to each other, we spent all Saturday night trying to kill ourselves with lovemaking, each resurrecting the other when we felt we had nothing left but find that reservoir virtually bottomless and we were rubbed raw in body yet as high as kites emotionally, declaring our undying love with every heaving breath as we tried to bring our pulse rates down to sustainable levels.

Chapter 10
Friday 15 May 1976, 3.15pm

I thought, no, I had quite simply assumed, that Gina was on birth control. We must've rung the bell while we were in Barcelona. Silly, careless me, leaving it all to Gina. Early in the spring Gina proudly announced that she was pregnant. She hadn't directly asked me, but she had determined that as we had discussed and agreed that children would feature in our future before Eric's death, and neither of us was getting any younger, so she just let nature run its course, hence the heavy and slightly unpredictable the periods of late.

I got down on my bended knee, as soon as the news of the baby sunk in, and I asked Gina to marry me.

She immediately said "Yes".

I asked Fred for her hand after the event and he gave it gladly. Pam's only comment, accompanied by a big smile and a hug, was, "You took your sweet time about it. But never mind, you make such a lovely couple, so give me a hug, Harry, and please call me 'Mum' from now on."

"Mum, Dad, thank you for welcoming me into your family. I have never felt so loved in all my life and I owe your family more than I can ever repay."

"Nonsense," Fred said, "you are family, son, and you've been an accepted part of us for so long that this marriage is simply confirmation of the fact."

We wanted a quiet wedding, but it far outgrew our ambitions, and it was Gina who persuaded my estranged son Gerald and my daughter Sophia Elizabeth and their own families to attend.

By then my Sophia Elizabeth was the size of a small house and I finally had a wedding day dance with her on our May wedding day after just a two-week engagement.

Gina and I had two lovely children together, Robert "Bobby" Alfred Crabtree, who was born in December 1976 and Margaret "Maisie" Eleanor Crabtree who first disturbed our good nights' sleep patterns in June 1979.

In 1996 I retired from the job of selling screws, nuts and bolts, but continued as a board member of King's and several other companies that I had been invited to join, through business contacts made over the years.

For King's, I was invited to monthly board meetings, attended the AGM and other get togethers in my own right as a director, as well as by being Gina's husband.

When Gina and Fred wanted me to join the board at King & Son, very much on a part-time basis, I spoke to my bosses in Birmingham and it turned out that most of the directors of my company served on several boards at the same time, without any conflict of interest. Through my new contacts with King's and Tremblett's I had picked up a lot of business, so my bosses encouraged me to accept the offer with their blessing.

I sat down with Gina and Fred and agreed that I would serve as a part-time member but my director's token remuneration would be donated to the different annual charity that the company chose and sponsored each year. I didn't want to be regarded as only in place because I was married to the female Chairman of the company. I also wanted to have a role or portfolio which would be my main contribution to the work of the board rather than just turn up for monthly meetings.

Fred thought I could formulate and keep updated all the policies of the company, regarding race relations, labour relations, disciplinary procedures, working practices, ethics, fair pay, emergency evacuations policy, security, etc, which I readily agreed to.

Over the years, with increasing legislation, there were more and more policies to oversee and that made me feel useful to the company, even long after I retired from full-time work.

Epilogue
Thursday 15 September 2005,

noon

I am enjoying my retirement and, although Gina still runs the Group as Chair person, she is gradually reducing her hours as my adopted son Giles Tremblett takes over more of the reins of power until she fully retires next year.

I see our son Bobby's two young children almost every day as they only live about eight miles from us.

Maisie was married last year to an airline pilot who flies long haul, so they are still living with us at the Manor House, but we have installed upstairs and downstairs internal locked doorways and a new "front door" into what used to be the mud room, which separates their suite of rooms so they can regard themselves as living independently. Maisie has a brand new modern kitchen and she often invites us to join them as guinea-pigs for her improving cooking skills. They are expecting their first child, Gina's third grandchild and my eighth, next spring.

I am driving my wife Gina in my original

1968 Silver Shadow, which has over 400,000 miles on the clock and it feels like a comfortable old glove to me.

We are off to enjoy a meal at the *Coach & Horses* to privately celebrate our first wonderful 30 years together. We have booked a room for the night, although the hotel part of the pub, an annexe added in the past twenty years, is hardly five star, it is the celebration of the event and the actual setting which matters, and means we can over indulge in our celebrations in all aspects of the word.

We are planning on celebrating our 30th wedding anniversary next year with all our large family and friends.

Gina has just bought me a brand new Phantom Rolls-Royce which was delivered a few days ago to celebrate the occasion. Of course I still wanted to use the car in which our relationship started and has continued unbroken since for our little annual celebrations.

Gina wanted me to have this new model and it is pretty fantastic and smells of newness, with every conceivable gadget and safety feature you'd need.

But it lacks the familiar majestic beauty that my Roller and my heavenly wife each have in spades, so I am sure I know which model I'll opt for when Gina and I have any future celebrations. Neither of the "old girls" in my life are ready for moth balling quite yet.

We exchange meaningful glances and smiles as I drive along the old familiar and quiet bypass, a road now superseded by the mighty ring road, and if in some ways life has passed us by as we enjoy less complicated lives, who cares?

With a glance from Gina full of promise and a mutual squeezing of our continually held hands, I believe the years have melted away from us and the Spirit of Ecstasy is alive and well and about to be put into practice again.

The End

Books by Tony Spencer

(all published on Smashwords.com unless specified; all paperbacks available on Amazon)

Novels
Lucky
Share Your Toys, Timothy! (also in paperback)
Jogging Memories (also in paperback)
Jake and Gill (also in paperback)
Bryan & Carla After the Supermarket (also in paperback)
The Archer's Apprentice (also in paperback)
Jen's Dream Santa (also in paperback)
A Blue Christmas (also in paperback)
The Archer's Lady (also in paperback)
Not Passing Go! (also in paperback)
One Shoe Gumshoe (due 2019)

Novellas
Fat Chance
Who Shot Father Christmas?
Know-Nothing Nigel
Rewind
When It Snows
ANJie
Nurses
It's All Gosford "Bloody" Tanner's Fault!
The Archer / The Chocolate Rose (also in paperback)
Dream Car (also in paperback)
The Extra (also in paperback)
The Spirit of Ecstasy

Short stories and collections

Fifty-Seven Fifty

Lane One Closure

Tea-Shop Twinkle

The One

Triptych of Couples (collection of 3 stories)

Shrinking Violet

The Telegram

Once Upon a Time ... The End? (collection of 7 stories)

Love Bites (collection of 52 stories) (also in paperback)

Fifty Shades of Monochrome (collection of 58 stories) (Amazon)

A Matter of Timing (on Wattpad)

Pass it on in the Mall (on Wattpad)

The Curious Case of the Horseless Headman (on Wattpad)

Spring Garden (on Wattpad)

The Dragonskin Chronicles (on Wattpad)

Bryan & Carla Bump Baskets (on Wattpad)

The Pre-Wake

A Night in Brighton

Cosmic Dustbunnies (a collection of about 26 stories due 2019)

Anthologies (also in paperback)

13 Bites vol III (The Curious Case of the Horseless Headman)

Collapsar Directive (Resolutions)

Other Realms (Two Realms, from *The Dragonskin Chronicles*)

Free For All (Hell on The Highway)

13 Bites vol V (The Pre-Wake)

Flash Fiction Addiction (The Foreigner)

The Author

TONY SPENCER is married, with two children and three grandchildren. Hailing originally from Wimbledon, Surrey, he has lived in Hampshire for fifty-five years, the last 35 in Yateley. He was a printer, typesetter and proofreader for over forty years. He has been writing sports reports for local newspapers for nearly half that time.

Tony started his first school magazine when he was 11 and been writing stories for hs own amusement ever since. He began sharing his writing and self-publishing fiction in 2012. He usually publishes a novel and several novellas each year.

He is always happy to receive feedback, so please contact him on tonyspencer1950@icloud. com

Printed in Great Britain
by Amazon